when he's BAD

NEW YORK TIMES BESTSELLING AUTHOR
LISA RENEE JONES

ISBN-13: 979-8579828422

Characters

Adrian Mack—34, goatee, dark wavy hair, six-foot-one. Hero of the story. Former FBI agent. Was once undercover with the Devils biker gang, and is now set to testify against Nick Waters, the leader of the gang. Now a prominent member of Walker Security.

Priscilla "Pri" Miller—32, brunette, blue eyes. Heroine of the story. Assistant District Attorney. Used to work for her father's law firm before she decided she wanted to put away the bad guys instead and went to work as an ADA.

Rafael—Younger brother to Adrian Mack. Rock star Latin singer.

Blake Walker—One of the three owning members/brothers of Walker Security.

Lucas "Lucifer" Remington—Walker Security team member. Blond, tattooed, rock god type looks. Pilot.

Savage—Walker Security team member. Former surgeon and special ops.

Dexter— Walker Security team member.

Adam— Walker Security team member.

Kirk Pitt— FBI agent, was undercover with Adrian. Handsome face, big and broad.

Ed Melbourn—District Attorney. Pri's boss. 50's. Fit, a big man, with thick salt-and-pepper hair, broad shoulders, and a broader presence. Single. Ex-military.

Nick Waters—King Devil, club founder, 42, brutally vicious, sports a dark beard with hints of gray, but doesn't drink or do drugs. He just peddles drugs, weapons, and women, while pumping iron, and adding new tattoos. Green eyes.

Grace—Pri's co-worker. 30, blonde, green eyes, in a relationship with Josh, shy.

Josh—Used to be the detective for the DA's office, but now has turned to private sector work. In a relationship with Grace. Light brown hair, strong, classically handsome features.

Jose Deleon—Waters' right-hand man, his assassin, most likely responsible for the murders of the witnesses.

Cindy—Newest ADA, straight out of school, petite, feisty, pretty blonde.

Logan Michaels—Pri's ex-fiancé, works with her father still. blond pretty-boy, clean-shaven jaw. Cheated on Pri with her secretary.

Shari—DA's office receptionist.

Mr. Miller—Pri's father. Owns his own firm. Pri used to work for him, Logan still does.

Mrs. Miller—Pri's mother. Wants Pri to come back to their family firm, refused to go out of town to stay safe during the case Pri is working on.

Dear Reader

Thank you so much for diving into Adrian's Trilogy! Book two in a trilogy is always more difficult for me. I'm so close to giving everyone (characters and readers alike) closure, but there's always so much more to delve into and experience. It's also usually the more emotionally tumultuous of the books. It's where the main characters discover so much more of each other, and I hope that bleeds through on these pages you're about to read.

But before you get to them, I wanted to give you a brief recap of book one, When He's Dirty. When we first met Adrian, though he was a solid part of Walker Security, he's also headed back to Austin, TX to finally testify in a case he was undercover in two years ago. A case that wholly changed his life forever. A case that made him a man he didn't recognize, and didn't want to be. He was undercover in the Devil's biker gang, and he's testifying against none other than the King Devil himself, Nick Waters. Waters is up for an entire slew of charges, violent and financial.

But before Adrian can testify, he needs to ensure the ADA on the case, Priscilla Miller, is on the up and up. Waters' reach is far and wide, he has any number of government officials under his control, and Adrian can't risk Priscilla being one of them. They meet under the guise of happenstance, and he introduces himself as his brother, Rafael. But as Pri (as Adrian calls her) dives deeper into the case, she unearths connections she can't fathom, and it suddenly becomes clear who Adrian really is.

As they get closer while trying to find out who is killing Pri's witnesses, they find this undeniable passion they can't say no to. But their closeness rattles a bunch of cages of those close to Waters, seemingly including Pri's ex-fiancé, Logan, who still works for her father's firm. Pri and Adrian are clearly getting too close to officially putting a nail in the coffin of this case and thus go into hiding at a cabin Adrian's father put together as a hideout many years back. But once they're settled and sleeping a visitor shows up, Agent Pitt, who was undercover with Adrian in the Devils, and he's soon stabbed by none other than Jose Deleon, Waters' right-hand man, who he tasks with all murders. Including the murder of Adrian and Pri. And thus, we're back at that cabin with Deleon threatening the life of Adrian and Pri...

Chapter One

ADRIAN

Impossible.

Deleon cannot be here at the cabin, at the hideaway I've told no one about but my team at Walker Security. And yet, here he is, big, tattooed, and smirking like the clown he is, but he's not just a clown. He's a killer, one who enjoys the sport of it.

Before Pitt ever hits the ground, with Deleon's knife buried in his back, Deleon charges at me. I reach for my gun, but before I can get off a shot, there's a blast at the rear of the house. My first thought is Pri, please God, do not let Pri be dead in the middle of one of my booby traps. But thank fuck, she screams in reaction to the blast, right here in the cabin, but I've hesitated with my fear for her, and it's a mistake.

Hesitation is the kiss of death with Deleon.

With a tackle, he takes me down, the hard floor punishing my back and jolting my bones and he doesn't do it silently. He's cursing me in Spanish, calling me a traitor and pig, but I don't miss another beat. I punch him. He punches me. I'm about to elbow the fuck out of him and flip us over when I hear, "Get off him or I'll shoot!"

Pri.

Holy fuck, Pri.

Deleon smirks at me, his long dark hair in disarray, half in and half out of the tie at his nape. His gun shifts, lifts, points at Pri, but he's still looking at me. "Make one little move," he promises, "and I'll shoot her before she shoots me."

"She's gutsy and well trained," I warn. "I wouldn't gamble against her skills or willingness to kill you."

"Are you really going to gamble against me?" he demands, smirking again, as if he knows I won't, but he doesn't shoot me or Pri.

Why, I wonder, did he bother to tackle me? Why not shoot me and be done with it when he had the chance? All I know are two things right now: I want his attention off Pri and I hope like hell she just shoots the fucker.

"What do you want, Deleon?" I demand softly.

His eyes burn with hatred. "Does your bitch know all the dirty shit you did, man? Does she know you're like us?"

"Isn't that exactly what makes me such a damn good witness?" I taunt, but I don't like where this is going.

"Does she know you killed your brother? Does she know you enjoyed it?"

That's it. I'm done. Adrenaline and anger collide in a surge. I roll him over, smash him to his fucking back, knock away his gun, and my blade is already in my hand. I don't even hesitate. I slam the damn thing into his chest, a non-lethal location just below his collarbone. But it hurts like hell and I know from experience that it bleeds like the bitch he is. He gasps, blood spurting from his mouth, and I'm already standing, rolling him to his stomach, my boot between his shoulder blades.

My gaze rockets to Pri, who's standing in the hallway, staring at me, her face pale, stricken. She's

6

looking at me like I'm a killer and she's not wrong, but it still burns the fuck out of me.

"He didn't come alone," I tell her. "Which means we have a few options here. We let his men come and kill us, I shoot him and kill him, or you grab me the rope under the kitchen sink so I can tie him up and you do it quickly."

Deleon quakes under my foot, trying to break free, and Pri darts for the kitchen. I stab Deleon again, just inside the shoulder blade, though I'd like to puncture his fucking lung. Then he'd be dead and *that* I'd enjoy, but it would also look like I did it to shut him up. I'd never come back from that with Pri. I'm not sure I can now anyway.

By the time Deleon gasps and collapses on the ground, Pri's handing me the rope. I glance at her pale features, but she's not looking at me. I guess she can't bear the sight of me, and it's starting to piss me off. I grab the rope.

"You stabbed him again?" she asks staring at the knife in Deleon's back and then gaping at me. "*You stabbed him again?*" she asks again.

Sure, I think, *now* she's looking at me and with accusations aplenty.

"He's alive," I say, unrolling the rope. "Check Pitt for a pulse. "

She draws in a breath and gives a choppy nod, rushing away. I knot the hell out of Deleon's wrists and make damn sure he's not going anywhere.

I rotate, grab my gun, and shove it in my pants. Pri's presently using tape and one of my T-shirts from the overnight bag to stop Pitt's bleeding, which tells me what I need to know. He's alive. He's also in the doorway. "I have to move him," I say. "We need to shut

7

the door." I don't wait for her reply. "Call Savage. Tell him Pitt's condition. *Now.*"

"I have to finish wrapping—"

"*Now,* Pri, or someone is walking through the door and killing us." I grab her arm and pull her to her feet, pressing the cell into her hand. "On speaker," I add.

She nods and I grab Pitt's feet, dragging him further into the cabin, blood pooling around his body as Pri punches in the call. Savage answers on ring number one. "We're ten minutes out," he announces.

"It's Pri," she says, kneeling next to Pitt again, and setting the phone on the ground. "Pitt showed up here at the cabin," she adds, applying pressure to his wound. "Deleon stabbed him. He's bleeding badly."

"Pitt?" Savage snaps. "And fucking Deleon? What the hell? Where's Adrian?"

I shut the front door and lock it. "I'm here," I say, kneeling next to Pri and taping up Pitt's wound. "We're going underground, so listen up because I'm leaving you a shit show."

"I love a good shit show," Savage jokes. "Bring it."

"I stabbed Deleon and tied him up," I say. "I saved his vital organs. We need to save him and turn him against Waters."

"He's alive?" Savage wonders. "I thought you wanted him dead?"

My eyes meet Pri's as I respond with, "You have no idea how fucking much I want him dead."

Pri cuts her gaze, a rejection in the action I feel like a blade in my heart. I stabbed Deleon, it's true, but there is no question he struck first, cutting me via Pri, and he knew it.

"All righty then," Savage says. "He's alive. We want him dead. What else?"

"That wasn't an invitation to kill him," Pri snaps. "I need him alive."

"No one needs that bastard alive," Savage grumbles, but he says, "Note to self: keep the piece of shit alive. Got it. What else?"

The alarm at the right side of the house sounds and I disconnect the call, launching myself to my feet while Pri, now covered in blood, smartly scrambles for her weapon.

"What's happening?" she calls out, gripping it and scanning the rear of the cabin.

"We need to go," I say. "That's what's happening."

Pri hesitates on the "we." It's in her face, her body language, her damn energy. "Adrian—"

"I will pick you up and carry you out of here if I have to," I promise her, not leaving room for her questions or contempt when I'm trying to save her life. "You decide." Another alarm sounds and this one is trouble, this one tells me how close trouble runs, which is too close. There's an explosion, a tripwire booby trap has been set off, which has Pri yelping while our enemy is waylaid at least for now. I grab her hand and start walking.

She doesn't fight me, at least not now, but thanks to Deleon, I know she will.

Chapter Two

ADRIAN

Our destination is the cabin bedroom, where I yank up the rug by the bed and pull open a hidden door. All the while my mind is processing the situation at hand. Only a handful of close people knew about this cabin. Those people include family, and the Walker team, who I just told, and yet somehow, Deleon and Pitt knew. That doesn't make me feel good about the tunnel we're about to enter, but we really have no options.

There's a crash at the front of the cabin, and Pri gasps and flattens against me. Certain that blast was the door being blown off, I pull her toward the steps leading into the tunnel. "Go! Go! Go!" I order.

She rushes into the darkness and I follow. With a practiced effort, I shut the door and flip the rug so that it falls back into place. Pausing at the top of the wooden steps, I grab the flashlight lodged on a piece of wood in the dirt wall and turn it on. Pri is at the bottom of the steps and I join her, eager to get moving down the narrow path. The less time we're in this hole, the better.

She grabs my arms. "I'm claustrophobic, very claustrophobic. I'm—bad. It's bad." She sways.

I catch her around the waist and mold her close. "Easy, sweetheart. Don't go down on me now. We have to move."

"I'm trying." She buries her face in my chest. "I'm trying. I just—" She looks up at me. "I fell in a hole as a kid. I have triggers. They're rare but—apparently," she makes a choked sound, "another hole is one of them. I'm sorry. I hate that I'm this weak."

I cup her face. "You are not weak and I understand, I do. But Pri—"

"I know," she says. "We're in a hole. We have to get out of the hole. I need to shake it off."

And there she goes, proving me right: she's not weak. "A half-mile," I say. "That's all you have to make it, but we have to go now. I don't know how Deleon found us, but if he knew about the cabin, he could have known about the tunnel. Outside of me, and until I told Walker, Rafael was the only living person who knows about it.

"How *did* Deleon know?"

"That's a question for later," I say, when the truth is that I feel certain it was my older brother, the one Pri doesn't know about. The one who is now dead. Alex, who was not only a dirty Fed, he became a Devil. "A half-mile," I repeat. "You walk further to work every day."

"I know," she breathes out. "I know." Without further ado, warrior princess that she is, she rotates forward.

One of my hand settles on the low ceiling and the other at her waist, letting her know I'm here, I'm at her back. I shine the flashlight over her shoulder, lighting our path and she starts walking.

I'm calm, my pace even with hers, but adrenaline pulses through me, and because Pri matters to me, I'm focused on how we get out of this alive. Even if Deleon knows about the tunnel, Walker is protecting us, and the exit isn't easy to find.

Pri and I fall into silence, walking forward, but Pri's breathing is raspy and too shallow. We're about halfway to the exit when I halt her and lean into her. "You've got this. *We've* got this."

"I can't seem to catch my breath."

"Just breathe in, sweetheart, long and full. Remind yourself you can do it."

She inhales, pulling in the breath, and my hand slides to her belly. "Now breathe out."

Her breath gushes from her lips. "I'm good," she hisses. "I'm fine. Let's go. Let's get out of here."

My lips curve with approval. "Let's go."

She steps forward, and I have no idea how she just defeated her demons, but I need lessons because she's in full charge, now in control of her baggage. With our new pace, we're at the exit quickly and I catch her hand, pulling her around to face me. "I need you to stay here while I clear the path. You have your gun?"

"In my purse." She pats it at her hip. "I grabbed it when I grabbed my gun."

"Pull it out and use it if you have to, but take my lead. Got it?"

"Yes."

I rotate us in the small space, pressing our bodies close as I take the lead. When I'm in front, she grabs my arm. "Do *not* get killed. We have things to discuss, you and me."

She's right. We do. Things like those times when I'm bad. And it happens far more often than she wants to know.

13

Chapter Three

ADRIAN

I head up the steel steps implanted in the tunnel wall, but pause at the top, just beneath the door. Smart man that my father was, he'd placed our exit location in the center of a circle of bushes, but that coverage does me no good if someone's waiting on us above.

For just a moment, I consider swinging back to the cabin, but I talked to the Walker team before we ever left Austin. We have a plan. They know my underground location and if the coast were clear to return to the cabin, they'd drop a light in the tunnel as a signal. And since that hasn't happened, I can only hope we're safe ahead.

Drawing my Glock, I ease the sliding door aside just enough to do a survey of what is directly in front of me and above, which is rain, a pounding, steady rain. The only good thing about rain, at least at this particular moment, is the extra coverage it offers. No one is standing in this downpour indefinitely. No one will have exceptional visuals as we make our getaway.

I glance down at Pri. "Be ready for a shower. It's a fucking downpour."

"Better rain than bullets," she murmurs.

Amen, I think. She's not wrong. I slide the door wider, and hitch upward on my hands, into the downpour. I'm instantly drenched and trying to spy our enemy in what is near zero visibility. I lift myself out of the hole and rest in a squatting position, waiting for a war that doesn't come.

Easing closer to the bushes, I'm up on my haunches, avoiding the booby traps I have set, creeping around the circle. I'm visualizing our path out of here as much as possible. The open clearing we have to travel on our way to the heavily wooded area beyond is a downside to my father's chosen path. He ran into issues with tree roots that forced him to end in that circle of bushes.

For now, there's no evident danger, but that doesn't mean it doesn't exist.

Eager to get us to a safe shelter, I return to the door to find Pri peeking out, scanning the area with her gun, offering me cover. And she dared to call herself weak. Holy hell, I've only known Pri for a few weeks and I think I want to know her for the rest of my life. Which won't happen. I've always known that's not how this ends. That's not how *we* end.

Staying low, I close the space between me and her and help her out of the hole, the rain instantly plastering her hair to her face. Motioning for her to stay where she is, I reseal the door, covering it with mud and foliage. With both of us in squatting positions, I face Pri, and the rain is so damn loud I signal with my hands to tell her to stay with me, stay silent, and stay down.

Once she nods her understanding, I motion to the two bushes free of booby traps, our safe exit point, and fuck me, I'm drowning. Our feet slush a path through muddy terrain in that direction, and I catch Pri's arm, holding her in place as I scan for a threat. I can't *see* any sign of trouble or anything else for that matter, and I can only pray that means trouble can't see us.

I wave two fingers forward and exit the bushes with Pri quickly by my side, both of us running through the wide-open space we can't avoid. Our path is the dark haven of trees and brush, a vertical horror house of obstacles, but a familiar one I welcome more than I dread.

We live if we survive those woods.

Chapter Four

ADRIAN

The night is dark and thank fuck my memory is not. We enter the forest, branches biting at our legs, but I've run this ground and I know every inch of the path we travel the way a blind man learns his own home. I hold onto Pri, ensuring she stays on her feet, navigating trees and rocks in absolute fucking darkness. The storm is plummeting down on top of us, a blanket of water that might as well be rocks. And still, we plod forward.

Once we're a good mile from the tunnel exit, I pull the flashlight from my pocket where I've stored it, keeping it low, pointing it at the ground. And I keep us in a forward momentum, determination in my every maneuver ahead.

In the process, my mind tracks in and out of the past, four and a half years ago in the past to be exact— the last thanksgiving my parents were alive. It was as always, a day that was all about family, and a spectacular meal my mother prepared, the chowing down process happening right before we decorated the tree. For a moment, I'm back at the dinner table. *This holiday it's just me, Mom, Dad, and Alex. Raf is halfway around the world on a tour, having scored a spot as an opening act for a big pop star.*

"I'm so glad you boys could be here," my mother says, scooping up another one of her famous tamales and setting it on my plate. I love these damn tamales. And I love the way her brown eyes light when Alex holds out his plate as well.

"More, Mom," Alex says. "Your boys miss your cooking."

Mom quickly obliges his request and fills his plate while my father laughs. My father loves this holiday time as much as we do. "I'm excited for Rafael," Mom says after we all dig into our food again, "but I miss him so much this year. It's off not having him here."

The longing in her voice that day still haunts me. Missing that holiday still haunts Raf. Nothing haunts Alex. He's dead, and apparently still proving he can fuck me over.

Pri trips and I catch her waist, holding her close, angry at my dead brother for playing a role in how she got here. Alex betrayed more than just me by giving up the cabin. He betrayed our promise to our father to treat the cabin as a family secret, our sanctuary.

When I'm certain Pri's solidly on her feet, I catch her hand again and do the best thing I can to protect her. I get us moving again toward my sanctuary, the one I created after my parents were murdered. Someone betrayed my father, the way Alex betrayed me. My father, my hero, who was skilled and intelligent, fell to the enemy, one we never named. It's a cold reminder to keep my guard up, and one that probably saved my life the night Alex died. *No*, I think, *the night I killed Alex.*

The rain wanes, but my anger and memories don't. I'm back in the past again, back to that same Thanksgiving, the last Thanksgiving with my parents. When dinner was done, another tradition kicked in.

Me, Alex, and Dad, all three of us FBI agents, headed out to the cabin, in what would be, as it always was, a chance to test our skills. One might think that made sense, us without Rafael, but we'd never been to the cabin without Rafael. For a long time, I'd wondered if his absence was why that day had felt off. Later, I knew better. Alex was off.

I'm back to replaying that day, to what told me he was off. We were at the back of the cabin where my father had designed a firing range and an obstacle course. I fade into the memory.

"Let's see what you're made of, boys," my father says, motioning us to the stacked bundles of hay. My father's a good-looking man, with tattoos on his arms, and a salt and pepper mix of thick hair.

Obediently, Alex and I line up behind the hay, ready to run the course.

Alex glances at me, a challenge in his eyes. "You want me to show you up first or last?"

I smirk. "Go for it," I say, because yeah, he's older, but I know my practice has paid off.

"Watch and learn, little brother," he says and there is something in his tone I can't quite name, but it's my decision to make. I'm not coddling him today. I'm whipping his ass.

He masters the course with impressive skill and time, gloating as my father cheers his performance. I'm up next and I perform with the ease of a man who's spent extra time out here that Alex hasn't. When I'm done, beating him by considerable standards, I don't gloat. I simply say, "How about a beer?"

Alex scowled at me, and to this day, I remember a glint in his eyes I'd never seen before. I didn't understand it then, but I do now.

It was hate.

He hated me. I'm pretty sure he hated us all.

A loud clap of thunder jolts me out of my own head, and I can almost imagine it as my father, a roar of his distress over one of us killing our own. And yet, I did. I killed Alex.

Pri and I near the end of this section of the woods and another clearing we have to pass through to get to the safe zone. This will be the final obstacle I anticipate between us and our destination. The sky seems to know, too, groaning and then opening up and blasting us with another downpour. That downpour, I decide, is a blessing, offering coverage we might not otherwise have at our disposal.

I halt Pri at the line of the woods and pull us to a squat behind heavy foliage and flip off the light, shoving it into my pocket. For a good two minutes, I scan the surrounding area, looking for trouble that I know can't be here. No one knows where I'm headed but Walker Security.

I lean into Pri and cup her head, lips at her ear. "Once we start running, do not stop for any reason."

She nods and I scan one last time before I motion us forward and we dart into the clearing. Adrenaline pumps through me. I pull Pri forward, ahead of me so I'm the target of any bullet that goes flying. It starts to hail, pelts of ice punching at us, and Pri stumbles again. I catch her before she goes down and she rights her footing and like a good little soldier, keeps moving. The run is short, but it's as if it's in slow motion, never-ending.

In my mind, I'm back in time again, living the moment after I killed my brother, and it's absolute hell. Everyone close to me dies and somehow in my mind, it's Pri lying there on the floor where my brother had died, Pri dying, like it's a damn premonition.

There's a crack in the air, a gunshot in the far distance. Pri reaches the woods on the opposite side of the clearing and, heart pumping, I'm right there with her. I catch her arm and step behind the wide column of a tree trunk and rest my back against it, pulling Pri in front of me. A second later, I rotate her, pressing her back to the tree, and sheltering her here in the dark stormy night, my body her armor, waiting for the bullets to fly.

LISA RENEE JONES

Chapter Five

PRI

Adrian's big body is a wall that halts the onslaught of rain, but who's protecting him? I know I heard a gunshot and I hold my breath, afraid for what comes next. Afraid he's sheltering me at his own peril. Afraid he will soon fall to the ground, injured or dying, like Agent Pitt. I don't know what happened with Adrian's brother and right now I don't care. I know we're out here, fighting for our lives, the two of us. And I know I wouldn't be alive right now if not for him. And I know he matters to me. Deeply, beyond what perhaps he should in a few short weeks, but I don't care about that either.

Thunder rumbles overhead and I lose track of time, fifteen minutes pass, I think, and we don't move. Finally, with no more shots fired, Adrian inches back from me, the rain slowing, almost a tease that promises more to come. He's still close, so close that I could almost forget we're in danger. Suddenly, one of his hands is on my head. I grab his T-shirt and now we're both holding each other and our weapons. He leans in again and his mouth slants over my mouth. And then he's kissing me, and it's not just a kiss. It's ravishing, hungry, a kiss that's pure obsession and even torment, almost a goodbye like he has to taste me once more before we die. I'm panting when his lips part from mine and he whispers, "We have to move."

Those words shouldn't comfort me, but the kiss did and the very fact that we're not dodging bullets, does. The very fact that we're alive and well and still able to run does, too.

"I need you to hold onto me," he says, taking my gun and sliding it into the back of my pants. "It's too dark to hold onto it and me."

I nod and he's already holding my hand, stepping back, the rain's retreat ending, as it pounds down on me, on us, once again. And then we're repeating the past hour, hiking through utter rain-laden darkness that feels almost as suffocating as that tunnel.

I'm exhausted when we start an upward, tortuous climb, but at least the terrain is smooth rock now, easier to maneuver. For a good ten minutes, we power upward, when to my relief, Adrian halts and pulls out his flashlight. It's then that I realize we're at the entrance to a cave and we're going inside. I have no idea why that concept doesn't freak me out, but I've learned over the years that there is no obvious rhyme or reason to my triggers. Or maybe I'm just too tired to have triggers right now.

Adrian motions for me to stand under a ledge of rocks. Once I'm in position, out of the rain, he bends over and enters the cave. I'm drenched and suddenly cold. Hugging myself against my shivers, I count down two full minutes before he exits and motions me forward. He squats down in front of the entrance and I join him. "It's narrow," he whispers, "but once you enter the main cavern, there's standing room and I've turned on a lantern."

I try not to think about the narrow part. I don't ask about the lantern or obvious planning he's done, either.

Not now. As he said, questions are for later. For the time being, I just nod and sway toward the cave's entrance. Adrian catches my arm. "You okay?" I hate that he fears my freak-out. I hate that I let him see me freak out at all.

"Yes," I reply and say nothing more. More feels like too much right about now.

He studies me a moment and I don't know what he expected to find and actually does find, but whatever the case, he releases me. I waste no time settling onto my hands and knees and entering the cavern. The path curves right and left. This ends at a decent-sized hole I climb through and I don't give myself time to panic. I suck in air and just go for it. It's not too tight and I'm through in an instant, but there's another hole to my left. I repeat my efforts, sliding through it, and then I'm there, on my knees, just inside a small, bedroom-sized cave aglow with the promised lantern. There's also a blow-up mattress, blankets, and what looks like a few boxes of supplies that must have taken real effort to get in here.

Adrian joins me and helps me to my feet, his hand only momentarily on my waist, steadying me, somehow branding me. He's been touching me the entire time we've been on the run in the woods, but somehow now I'm not immune, not even close. How can I be? He, unlike me I'm sure, looks good with his T-shirt clinging to his muscled chest and his dark hair plastered to his handsome, if not weary, face. Not to mention, the taste of that passionate kiss we'd shared in the woods still lingers on my lips despite the rain trying to wash it away.

"Home sweet home until our rescue squad arrives," he says, giving me a concerned inspection. "How are you doing in here?"

"Fine," I say and while I'd like to leave it at that, and forget my panic attack happened, I doubt he can forget, not under these confined circumstances. He needs more from me than one word. I rotate to face him and say, "It's hard to explain, but the triggers are random, unpredictable, and infrequent. And at present, I think I'm too tired, cold, and numb to feel anything but relief to be anywhere but out there in the rain."

He's back to studying me with a far too keen eye, and I can feel the tug of a question he isn't asking between us. And I know why or I think I do anyway. I believe he's afraid that if he asks questions that I answer, I'll then ask him questions, and he'll feel obligated to answer me.

He doesn't risk the quid pro quo I wouldn't demand and actually don't want to extend myself on this particular topic. Instead, he reaches over and strokes my wet hair from my face, tenderness in his touch that defies a man capable of killing his brother—that is unless he had no choice. I catch his hand, silently letting him know that I still believe in him.

If he really killed his brother, I know in my gut that he had no choice. And he certainly didn't enjoy it.

He cuts his gaze, his expression hidden from view, but not before I glimpse the shame and regret in his eyes. Not before I see the truth. He killed his brother, I'm certain. At this point, that part isn't a surprise, but I saw something else in his expression. Something I can't name. Something even beyond the obvious that he doesn't want me to know right now or I suspect, ever.

Chapter Six

PRI

There's a heavy beat between me and Adrian that he doesn't allow to last. "Let me get you a towel and some dry clothes," he says, and then he's moving away from me, putting what space there is to garner between us.

He crosses the cavern and squats down near a row of boxes sitting against the wall. "For you," he says, tossing a towel at me, which I catch easily and accept eagerly.

"How do we know Waters' men can't find us here?" I say, doing what I can to dry off considering I have water literally dripping from my clothes. "They found the cabin."

"No one knows about this place but Walker." He scrubs his hair with a towel. "And I only told them about it yesterday."

"Deleon found the cabin," I argue, closing the space he's put between us and squatting down beside the mattress.

"No one but me knew about this cave until yesterday," he says, "when I told my Walker team. "

"You said no one knew about the cabin."

"No one that I thought could, or would, hurt us," he says. "That was a misstep. I fucked up."

"How do we know Walker didn't turn on you?"

"They didn't." He digs in a box and sets socks, a T-shirt, and sweats on the mattress, obviously done with the idea of Walker turning on him. "Those are for you," he says. "I have safety pins for the sweats." He reaches in another box and sets a small box, that I assume holds the pins, on top of the stack of clothes.

I ignore the clothes, not ready to allow him to change the subject. "Someone told Deleon, Adrian."

"It wasn't Walker. You're shivering. Get out of those wet clothes."

Somehow, I never thought being ordered out of my wet clothes by this particular man would ever feel cold and commanding, more than hot and commanding, but it does. He's using it to shut down my questions.

"I better keep on my pants, though, in case we have to leave suddenly. I mean, Savage could be here any minute, right?"

"Don't count on it," he says. "The storm and the darkness mean we're all safer waiting for morning. "

"Can you call him?"

"I dumped my phone at the cabin," he says. "I can't risk that somehow being how Deleon found us."

"I thought your phone was safe?"

"We have to be paranoid right now." He motions to a sheet hung up like a shower curtain, though I'm not sure, considering we're in a cave. "There's a portable toilet back there."

I glance at the sheet in surprise and then back at him. "You really thought of everything."

"Right before I went undercover with the Devils, I knew how dangerous the mission would be. I prepared for a moment like this one and hoped it wouldn't come."

And I can't help but wonder what role his brother Alex played in this, but I give up on seeking answers.

He's not ready to talk. I can see that. I want him to know I get it, I understand, even if it's killing me. "Adrian—"

He stands and strips his wet T-shirt over his head, his hard, tattooed body now on full display, my words lost, my mouth dry.

"You wanted to say something?" he asks, but his tone is as cold as him commanding me to undress. I have the impression he's just used that tone and his state of undress to distract me, even manipulate where my head is right now. Despite truly understanding why he might do so, why he's so worried about the question I might ask, I don't like this. I don't like how he's making me feel.

Suddenly needing the same space his words and actions declare he needs, I scoop up the clothes. "I'll use the bathroom and change," I murmur, rotating as I stand. In a couple of steps, I'm behind the curtain and I'm not sure if that is good or bad. I've basically just told him that I won't undress in front of him.

I don't know what is happening between us right now.

Chapter Seven

PRI

Standing behind the sheet, I draw a deep breath and bring the makeshift bathroom into view. There's a portable toilet, a trashcan, and even a mock sink made from a bowl with soap and bottled water. A small box of supplies sits beside it and includes toothpaste and brushes. The man has covered it all, I decide, and I wonder what it was like to be undercover, in a situation so dangerous you needed a hideout in a cave. There are layers of torment to this man hidden beneath all of his jokes. This cave proves it.

I quickly dry off and change, after which I feel a ton better just wearing dry, albeit excessively large, clothes. As for my discarded, soaked items, my bra included, I hang them on the clothes rack—yes, there is a portable folding clothes rack. This place is like a well-stocked apartment.

Ready to rejoin Adrian, I'm nervous when I've never been nervous with him, thus my deep, calming breath, before I step into the main cavern. I find Adrian fully dressed in fresh, dry clothes, sitting on the mattress, his back against the cavern wall, his long legs stretched in front of him, his booted feet crossed. His body is perfect. His dark hair is damp, his handsome face schooled in an unreadable expression.

His eyes, those warm brown eyes, slide over me, lingering on the pucker of my nipples beneath the white tee that I've knotted at my waist. Heat and a mix of confusing notions stir in my belly and when his gaze lifts and collides with mine, there is a charge in the air that is as electric as it is familiar and welcome.

"I'm making hot chocolate," he says, indicating the camping stove where a pot sits on top.

"How is that even possible?" I ask.

His lips curve, the hint of a smile easing the tension between us. "You don't camp much, do you?"

"Once," I say. "When I was twelve. All I remember is waking up with about a hundred mosquito bites on my forehead."

He laughs. "That many, huh?"

"Yes!" I assure him. "I'm not joking, but," I add, holding up a finger, "we did make s'mores on an open flame. I remember that fondly."

"Now we make hot chocolate with propane." He pats the mattress. "Come sit, Pri." His voice is as warm as cocoa while our connection has somehow become as sticky as the marshmallows on that fire so long ago. Proven by him adding, "*If* you want to."

That very statement or question, I'm not sure which, drives home the stickiness between us that was not present before Deleon showed up. In mere minutes, that monster built a wall Adrian and I must now tear down. Me changing behind that curtain added bricks, made it wider and taller. I don't like it. I don't welcome it. We've given Deleon too much power.

I want it back.

We need it back.

I join Adrian, sitting down on the edge of the mattress, not right next to him, but not on the opposite end of the inflated cushion either. "I can't believe you were prepared enough for this to have hot chocolate in a cave."

"And coffee and M & M's," he assures me. "Essentials matter."

"Is this where you tell me a goofy joke about coffee?" I tease.

"No," he says softly, a small tic in his jaw. "I don't have a joke in me right now."

I pull my knees to my chest and rotate to face him. "You got him, Adrian. If we can make Deleon talk—"

"He won't talk," he says, his expression unreadable and when I would push for answers, some sort of timer goes off. "That will be the hot water," he announces, grabbing the pot and pouring water into two cups that must-have cocoa powder inside them.

He uses a wooden stir stick and swishes the contents of the cups and then hands me one. "Thank you," I say, accepting the cup.

Our fingers brush, our eyes colliding with a jolt, the air thickening between us. "What do you call sad coffee?" he asks.

My lips curve. "I don't know. What do you call sad coffee?"

"Depresso."

I laugh, a genuine laugh that defies the hell of the past few hours. "*That* is so *very* cheesy."

"But you laughed."

"I did," I say, and I don't point out that just minutes ago he didn't think he could tell a joke. I hope this means he's relaxing back into our relationship. I sip the warm beverage that is both sweet and yummy. "How did you find this place?" I ask.

"I was involved in a shooting that fucked me up," he surprises me by admitting. "I came up to the cabin and hiked to just clear my head. Ironically, it was raining that day and I took shelter here in the cave. The storm lasted for hours and I had gear with me and just started exploring the cave."

"When was that?"

"Five years ago, but I didn't turn it into a shelter until I agreed to go undercover with the Devils."

"Why create it at all if you thought the cabin was secure?"

"My father always told me to do better than him, be better than him. And definitely be better than my enemies."

"You were," I say, absoluteness in my tone. "*You are*, Adrian."

His lips tighten. "I told you—"

"You're dirty and bad," I supply, knowing this story already.

"Yes," he agrees, sipping his hot chocolate. "I am."

I could push him now, dive into the topic of Deleon, remind him he could have killed him, but the edge between us is only now fading. I decide Deleon's a stiff topic better eased into when we too are not so, well, stiff. Instead, I ask, "What was the shooting that upset you enough to seclude yourself out here?"

"A teenager. He drew on me. I had no choice, but his parents were good people. It destroyed them."

My gut twists just hearing the explanation and not because of the words. Because that's big and he shared it freely despite the fact that five years later, demons dance in the shadows of his eyes. My God, what is it that he won't tell me? Or at least dreads telling me? I don't know. I don't know if I want to know, but I have no doubt at this point that he looks in the mirror and sees a monster, not a hero. I choose to see a hero. He *is* a hero.

I sip the hot chocolate and set it aside, scooting across the mattress to sit next to him, leaning against the cavern wall. Mere inches separate us.

"Tell me about falling into a hole as a kid," he urges.

I glance over at him and lift the glass. "I might need wine."

"I have whiskey."

"If we stay in here long enough, I might need it," I joke, but then backtrack. "Actually, talking about my little incident doesn't really bother me. Not at all. In fact, I always feel like I'm over it and then I'll have some crazy reaction to something, like the tunnel. It sideswipes me and makes me angry at myself for having so little control." I wave my hands around the cavern. "I mean, why doesn't this bother me but the tunnel did?"

"It's small and the exits aren't easy to see and reach."

"True," I concede, "but I freaked out when I first got into the tunnel, and I could still see the exit."

"The exit we couldn't go through without ending up dead," he reminds me. "I think your mind has logic working for you. What happened when you were a kid?"

"My father had a big client in Texas. We spent the weekend at his ranch and I fell down a well. I broke an arm and a leg. It took them six hours to find me. I went through physical therapy, the whole gambit."

"Ouch," he grimaces. "That's wicked. How old?"

"Six. I honestly barely remember it, which is why it's hard to fathom why I still randomly have a reaction."

"The mind stores the trauma," he says softly, his lashes lowering and then lifting. "It's with you forever."

I have a flickering memory, a recent memory, a trigger in an unexpected, complicated place I shove aside. I focus on him. I need to focus on him. "Spoken like a man with experience."

He reaches into a box and grabs a bottle of whiskey, removing the cap and slugging back a swallow. That's his answer, his *only* answer and sometimes actions mean more than words. He offers me the bottle. I'm a horrible drinker, a truly horrible drinker but I take the bottle and slug it back, choking with the sharp pinch of the amber liquid.

Adrian laughs a deep, masculine rumble, and takes the bottle from me. "You okay?"

"As if you care. You laughed."

"I care despite my amusement."

"Hmm. Well. I think I should have stuck to hot chocolate."

"Why?" he challenges, taking another long slug. "You're in a cave with a devil. Drink."

"You're not a devil."

"I was," he says. "I had to be. And once a devil, always a devil."

"You didn't kill Deleon."

"For you." His eyes meet mine for just a moment before he tips the bottle to his lips and swallows, his chin tilting downward before he adds. "You don't know what I've seen him do." His gaze finds mine again, almost as if he wants, and even needs, me to see the truth in his face as he adds, "I would have killed him if you hadn't been there."

He means it, of that I'm certain. I take the bottle. "Then I guess we'd better hope I make that a good decision."

I force down another swallow, and this time, the burn delivers a hazy sensation, a lightheaded feeling. I tip the bottle back again in a repeat and the sensation intensifies. My words are looser now, my limits wider. "I imagine your trust is a shiny ball," I dare, bold enough to meet his stare as I add, "a prize I hunger to be awarded. Close enough to reach up and pluck from the darkness, only to have it dart just out of reach." I hand him the bottle.

He grabs it and for several beats he says nothing, staring at me, his expression indiscernible, a pulse in the air as he says, "It's not as simple as me just deciding to trust you, Pri."

I'm remotely aware of the drip-drop of water nearby, stone to stone, a simple, discernible act of nature much like our attraction. But as he's made clear, that is where simple ends for us.

But I am just whiskey'd up enough to plow forward, not in the slightest deterred from my mission, a mission I can only call *him*. I want him to stop seeing me as a person who will judge him instead of a woman who cares about him. "I haven't trusted anyone in a very long time," I say softly. "But I trust you."

"You think this is about trust, but it's not."

"Then what's it about?"

His jaw flexes. "The cold-hearted facts. I did things. Things you won't like."

"I did things, too," I remind him. "Things you won't like."

He sets the bottle down. "Pri, damn it—"

"Adrian, damn it," I snap back.

"You heard what Deleon claimed," he counters. "Why are you ignoring it?"

"I'm not ignoring it. You won't talk to me. Not without that immunity agreement. I get that."

"I will never talk about my brother." His voice is low, almost what you would call soft, and yet somehow it bands around the words and converts them to pure steel.

That steel cuts through the whiskey haze, but it doesn't shut me down. "You killed him," I say. "I know."

"How would you know that, Pri?"

"It's bleeding from you. You did it, but unlike what Deleon said, you didn't enjoy it."

"How do you know?"

"Because you had to come to the cabin to deal with killing a teenager you didn't even know. There's no way you weren't torn up over your own brother."

His response is to take a long drag of the whiskey before he sets it aside. The next thing I know he's laying me down, his big body pressed to mine. The delicious weight of him sends a surge of adrenaline pulsing through me. "You think you know me?"

My fingers curl on his cheek. "I know enough."

"And if you're wrong?"

"I think you're the one who's wrong," I counter.

He doesn't ask what I mean. His lips lower, lingering above mine, teasing me with a kiss not yet realized. "This right now," he says softly, "changes nothing."

And now, I don't ask what he means. I already know. His demons don't just dance in his eyes, they dance *with* us, they mock us. They promise to end us.

And what he doesn't understand is how little that matters to me. So much so that I can't wait to meet them up close and personal and tell them, and him, they don't matter. But he does. So fast, so easily, Adrian matters to me.

Chapter Eight

ADRIAN

I tell myself to get up, not to kiss her, not to hold her this close. The more I take from her, of her, the more she'll hate me for it later, and yet she'll hate me no matter what. And hate is hate.

Now is now and the rest can't be changed.

With a mental "fuck it" I decide now is all we're guaranteed, and my mouth closes down on Pri's. I lick deep, drinking her in, the sweet taste of whiskey, chocolate, and sin on my tongue. She moans and my cock thickens, my body a live charge of lust, and that's what I want this to be: lust, *just lust.*

Her fingers dive into my hair, tangling there, heat coursing through my veins, and I tell myself that this draw to Pri isn't just lust. It's about the forbidden. She's forbidden. We're crossing lines and I've learned I do that too damn well. I like living on the edge far too much and too easily.

I'm playing a dangerous game and doing it with the wrong woman. Pri will soon know too much about me, see too much of me, and I tell myself that's the draw. My desire for her is fed by a burn to live on the edge. I did it for so long that I don't know how to stop. Or maybe the truth is far more complex. All I know is that I want her more than I remember wanting anyone, ever.

"Adrian," she whispers, eager for me when she's too smart to go down this path, and yet she does with me. What the hell is she thinking?

She pants into my mouth, and my teeth nip her bottom lip, punishing it while my tongue laves the offended skin. She tugs at my T-shirt and I pull it over my head, tossing it aside, kissing her again, hard and fast, unable to wait for more. I always want more of her.

My fingers slide under the white tee Pri wears, *my* white tee, that's on her body. Warm, soft skin greets me and my hand finds her breast, teasing her nipple. She arches into my touch and I shove the cotton up just enough to bare her nipple, licking and sucking the pink puckered tip.

Her soft sounds of pleasure undo any resistance I have left as if I've ever had any with Pri. I drag the T-shirt over her head, my gaze raking over her perky naked breasts, my cock pressing against my zipper.

My mouth covers hers again and my hand slides under her backside, cupping her cheek, and molding all her soft, fuckable curves nice and close. We're fucking. This is us fucking, *just* fucking.

Her fingers dive into my hair again and tug roughly, and there it is, that side of her that tempts me in all kinds of dirty ways. She thinks she understands me, even knows me, but she hasn't even begun to see who I am. What I am. And damn it to hell, I want to show her. I want to show her and I want her to be able to handle it, but that's not what just fucking is about. Fucking is about not caring if she can handle it.

I pinch her nipple a little too hard, and she gasps in my mouth and repays the favor, her fingernails digging erotically into my arm. "You're afraid of me," she accuses.

Stunned, I pull back, our lips lingering a breath apart. "You're the one who should be scared."

"And yet, I'm not."

"You will be," I promise, and I don't give her time to push for more. I slant my mouth over hers and a wild, hot need erupts between us. I want my tongue all over her, I want to drive her wild, but the absolute physical need to bury myself inside her, to feel her warm and tight around me is just too fierce. My hands slide under her waistband and caress the oversize sweats down her legs, all the way down. I get rid of her shoes and socks as well, and then she is naked, her ivory skin flushed, while my heart is pounding.

Our eyes meet and there's a punch in my chest I have never known with another woman. She sits up, her arms wrapping my neck, and I lower myself over her. But I don't kiss her. I lean in and bury my face in her neck, inhaling her scent that is still somehow, impossibly fresh and feminine. She's naked, while I am not, still proving herself willing to be vulnerable, and at my mercy, and I don't know why. She is not naïve. She is not even close to naïve.

Suddenly, an urge to push her the way she wants to be pushed, the way I almost pushed her at the cabin overtakes me. I could make her see that darker side of me, but damn it, I'm not ready to let her go.

Her hand is on my face, her fingers in my hair, tugging me to her, and when I draw back, there's no going slow. Our mouths collide, and I'm cradling her to me.

"Adrian," she pants, and I know what she wants, what I want.

I don't even remember shoving my pants down, and then I'm sliding into the warm, snug heat of her body. I drive into her, and she gasps, arching into me. I catch her knee and drag it to my hip and thrust again and again. Low moans and pants fill the cavern until she's shuddering into release, her body spasming around me, dragging me with her.

When our bodies are calm, I roll off Pri and fix my pants before I grab her a tissue. In silence, she dresses, and damn it, we're awkward again. I don't even know how it happened. And I never even fully undressed. Maybe she thinks that's because I just couldn't wait to be inside her, which is true. Or that I need to be ready if we're attacked. Also true. Or maybe she thinks it's because fucking her just wasn't that important to me. Not true. Not even close to true. Right now, in this moment, it's time to admit it: Pri matters to me.

Too.

Damn.

Much.

Offering her privacy, claiming some for myself, trying to shake off whatever the hell this spell is that she's cast on me, I present her my back, legs cocked in front of me, wrists resting on my knees. Damn it to hell, what am I doing? I need a run. I need a shower. I need *her*. I need all those bad things I did to just go away.

But they won't.

"Already you regret that," she says, her voice a soft quake.

I rotate to face her to find her fully dressed and standing to the side of the mattress. Beautiful Pri. Smart Pri. Insightful Pri, but she's wrong this time. I stand and face her, the mattress in front of me and beside her. "I don't regret touching you, Pri. Never."

"Right," she says. "Just regret in general. I get it. I know all about regrets."

She turns away from me and disappears behind the sheet. I don't think. I just act. I follow her, rounding the

44

barely existing barrier just as she pulls the T-shirt over her head. I catch her elbow and tug her around to face me, her breasts bare, and already I'm hot and hard again.

"What are you doing?" she demands, covering her chest with the tee still in her hand.

"What are you doing?"

"Sometimes a girl feels more in control in a bra, even if it's a wet bra. I'm trying to put it on."

And I'd rather she not, I think, but what I say is, "I regret a lot of things, but you are not one of them."

"You giving me your back says otherwise."

"I was giving you privacy."

"Because willingly getting naked on a cavern floor says I need privacy?"

"You're back here, putting on a bra."

"I'm right here, half-naked in your arms again, Adrian. But yes, I need and want to put on my clothes."

"Let them dry." I grab the T-shirt from her hand and pull it back over her head. "We need to get some rest. Tomorrow will come early."

"And so will goodbye, right?"

A tic forms in my jaw. "You're stuck with me at least until after the trial."

"Stop it," she snaps. "Stop now."

"Stop what, Pri?"

"If you want to push me away, do it. If you believe that's what's right, do it. Because we both know that's what you're doing. Deleon convinced you our day of reckoning is coming, so you decided to rush it along.

"It is coming," I say. "It's already here."

"You mean you've already decided what I will think of you, and where my mind, heart, and regrets will be when this is over. You don't get to make my decision for me or think for me, for that matter. You don't have that right. Now I'm putting on my bra and pants. Now you can give me that privacy."

I feel that hard push away, and I don't like it. My hands gently shackle her waist and I step into her, my forehead lowering to hers. "Don't do this," I plead softly. "I know I deserve it, but," I ease back to look at her, "don't do this. Don't push me away."

She grips the T-shirt a little tighter in front of her and between us. "I don't know what you want from me, Adrian. And I don't have the emotional capacity to be this confused while fighting a war."

"I'm crazy about you," I confess, "like I have never been for another woman. I just don't fucking know how we end up together on the other side of this. And don't read some kind of intent into that."

"And I'm crazy about you, too, but every man in my life, including you, has tried to make my decisions for me. I'm done letting that happen."

"That's not what I'm trying to do."

"You've already decided what I'll feel about you when you testify. Because you think I can't handle the truth of your past."

"I know you can't."

Her eyes flash. "*I decide* what I can handle, and honestly, I don't know how I'll handle what you've done, I won't pretend I do. I can't know, but neither can you."

"I know," I insist. "*I know.*"

"What I know," she says, poking my chest, "is that lies hurt. Lies I can't take. Honesty matters to me."

"I have always been honest with you, Pri."

"I know. That's my point. Be honest with yourself and me right here, right now. I know we're in a cave together, but if you just want us to step back, to be all business—"

46

My hands come down on her arms. "I don't want that at all."

"Want and need are two different things. So maybe you don't want to step back, but if you need—"

"No. I don't need to step back. I told you. I'm crazy about you, which is why I'm trying to do right by you."

"Right by me?" she asks incredulously. "What does that even mean?"

"I know the fair thing to do, the right thing, is to step back from us and stick to all business until this is over."

She gives my chest a hard shove and does just that, steps back. I let her when all I want to do is pull her close again. This reaction, this absolute need for her, is new to me and dangerous to her.

"You're right," she says. "All business is best. We broke rules. We crossed lines. I know." But there is a slight tremble to her bottom lip that says she doesn't know.

I don't know either.

But today has been a solid reminder that the ones I love end up hurt. Or worse, dead.

There are things I want to say to her, most of which start with "when this is over" but I stop myself. When this is over, she'll know who I really am, and this, *us,* will really be over.

I step around the sheet and leave her there, close enough to protect her, but too far away to touch.

Chapter Nine

PRI

The minute Adrian disappears out of sight, I collapse against the cavern wall and squeeze my eyes shut. Adrian just shut me down, pushed me away. And it hurts. Obviously, I fell hard for him.

And that is what I know.

What else explains the thundering of my heart beneath my hand now balled right at that tight spot between my breasts? What else explains the way I hang on his words, and welcome his touch when I have had no other in so very long? What else explains that even with murder and mayhem around me, he brings a smile to my lips without even trying. And what else explains just how affected I am by the way he's pushed me away?

Nothing, but I fell hard for him.

And now, he's pushed me away.

Logically, my sane, educated mind knows that's the smart thing anyway. I do. I completely understand that reality, but I'm back to my pounding heart beneath my fist. Back to how much it hurts. Still, I force my logical mind to take over again. He's damaged, deeply, perhaps irreparably damaged. He doesn't believe I can want him. He's protecting himself, and me. Nothing will change where we are right now, but full exposure, and I'm not even sure an immunity deal will be enough. I believe Adrian will wait as long as he can to talk to me and tell me as little as possible to make our case in court. Considering this is all going public, to be telecast live and in a big way, I can't blame him.

Bottom line, both of us need the war to be over. Both of us have put everything on the line to take down Waters, and I need to remember that, him more so than me. He will always be "that guy" once he testifies on national television. The best thing I can do for both of us is to convict Waters. That's my job, and that needs to be my focus. I push off the wall, and I'm remarkably calmer now. I'm focused. We're alive. We are on the right track to justice. Putting sexual tension aside, for now, is a good thing.

Resolved to focus on my duty, and taking down Waters is my duty, I determine a need to talk through my Deleon strategy with Adrian. With this in mind, I round the sheet, and Adrian's presence jolts me anew as if I wasn't just touching him. Just that easily he consumes me. He's on the floor, leaning on the wall, his long, powerful legs stretched before him, and he looks ruggedly male—so damn good looking. That's how it works for men. They can be muddy and weary and they just enhance the manly factor. For me, I'm pretty sure I just look like a wet mess.

Adrian's eyes meet mine, and mine his, no avoidance between us. There is no question the pulse of our attraction is alive and well, and yet that wall Deleon sought to build, stands stronger than ever.

I walk to the mattress and sit down, leaning against the cavern wall, a good two feet between us now that feels like a mile. On some level, I think Deleon won. On another, I decide he lost in a big way. He solidified my need to make the sacrifices so many have made to take him and Waters down, count.

My gaze slides to the gun on Adrian's left, and the bottle of whiskey in his right hand. "Drinking and a gun doesn't seem like a good idea," I dare.

"While in a cave with you," he says, "it's a perfect combination. Besides, my weapon is a part of me, an extension of who I am. Booze doesn't change that."

I inhale on a punch of emotions I cannot name, and my lashes lower, fingers curling by my sides. This push and pull between us is brutal. There's no cooling off between us, just different degrees and types of heat. He's already decided we're enemies, and I pray that's not true.

"Right," I say, and when I open my eyes, he's tilting back the whiskey.

I realize then that no substantial question I ask will be met with a productive answer, not tonight. "Do you have paper and a pen?" I ask.

He uses the whiskey bottle to indicate the boxes by the wall. "If we have it, it's in there."

We.

Well, at least "we" still exist in some way for him. I crawl to the boxes, find a pad and pen, and then return to my spot on the mattress against the wall. It's time to get focused. Tomorrow, if all goes right, I'll be pushing Deleon to roll over. Adrian might not think that's possible, but when someone faces life behind bars, something inside them shifts. In Deleon's case, we witnessed him stab a man who I pray is still alive.

My mind flashes with an image of Agent Pitt gasping for air, and then the blood, so much blood, pouring from his body. I have to make Deleon and Waters pay. I have a job to do and I am now officially focused on that job. I start prepping for that interview, writing down questions, strategies, angles. I don't know how much time passes, but my hand has cramped when I've finished five pages of notes. At this point, Adrian's head is resting against the wall, his eyes shut. That's where he's going to sleep. That's how much he wants to avoid me.

With a clench of my gut, I set my work aside and lie down, shivering with the damp cave and pulling a blanket over me. In that moment, I feel alone, which was far more comfortable before I met Adrian. Funny how one soul meets another and everything changes. He did the impossible. He found me and I didn't even know I was lost.

I'm just not sure I actually found him, or that I ever will.

Chapter Ten

PRI

The drip-drop of water once again echoes through the cold cavern. It's raining again. Maybe it never stopped.

I lie on the mattress and stare at the ceiling, certain I won't be able to sleep. Rolling over, I face Adrian and find his eyes are on me, and in the shadows of his stare there is a story to read, one with no happy ending. It's a story of torment, pain, and brutality and I realize he wants me to understand the latter, the brutality. As if he is done trying to hide it, only I already read this book, at least this dark chapter. I already know he's lethal and so is the gun next to him. What he doesn't understand, nor do I, is that it seems to work for me. In fact, I think it's because of these things, because I know he's a killer, that I'm able to shut my eyes. And when I do, the heaviness of a long day, a grueling physical and emotional explosion of a day, overtakes me. I shut my eyes and I'm back in the cabin, reliving it all. Pitt falling to the ground. Adrian and Deleon rolling around on the floor. Adrian stabbing Deleon. I was certain he was dead and for just a moment, I wished it were true. That's why I didn't immediately hand Adrian the rope. I thought Deleon was dead.

I glance over at Adrian and the bottle of whiskey is still in his hand. No help there to numb the events of the day. Not unless I want to take it from him, and I get the feeling he doesn't want to be bothered. I force my eyes shut and tell myself I have to sleep. I have to be fresh to interview Deleon. I start counting sheep, literally, for the first time in my life.

I obviously fall asleep because I wake with a start and jolt to a sitting position, scanning my surroundings only to realize I'm still in the cavern and Adrian is kneeling beside me. "Hey, sweetheart. Nothing's wrong. We're okay."

Sweetheart. The endearment is wildly unexpected and remarkably calming. "What's happening?" I whisper.

"My alarm happened," he says. "I set it for sunrise."

I throw away the blanket and pull my knees to my chest, my pulse leaping anxiously, the harsh need for more sleep gone in a blink. "That's when Walker will come for us?"

"If they can. We need to be ready."

My brows lift. "If they can?"

"Walker moves when it's safe. We don't know what's going on outside the cave."

Of course, he's right, I think. We don't even know if it's still raining. "Then what?" I ask, my mind instantly on the pages of notes I took last night. "What happens when Walker shows up?"

"We get the hell out of these woods."

"Right. Of course. Good." I shift to my knees to get up. "I need to pee, brush my teeth, and get my brain connected before I interview Deleon." I twist away from him, but he catches my elbow before I can stand.

The touch shocks me and if I wasn't wide awake before, I am now. Our eyes collide, and Lord help me, heat charges up my arm and across my chest. That is until he says, "Deleon is going to have to wait."

I blink. "Wait? What does that mean?"

"We're going to New York City."

"No," I say, pushing back. "I'm not going to New York. I have a job to do."

"And so do I."

I jerk out of his touch as if burned. "And I'm your job."

"You know that's not what I meant."

"Isn't it?" I challenge.

He scrubs a hand through his tousled hair. "What do you want me to say here, Pri?"

"You got me naked last night and then this morning I'm a job." My voice is pure contempt as I add, "I think you've said enough."

"You are not *just* a job." His voice is low, almost vehement.

"Okay," I concede. "Then we're friends, Adrian, but that doesn't mean—"

"Friends?" he demands, a crack to his tone. "Is that what we are?"

"Do you have a better description?"

"Complicated," he replies. "And catching Deleon doesn't mean Waters doesn't keep coming. He'll just send someone else to kill us. We need to step back and regroup."

"We need to end this," I say. "That means I need to get in front of Deleon before he clams up. Now. Not later."

"No," he says, the one word flat, simple. To the point.

I laugh without humor. "*No*? You can't tell me no."

"And yet, I am."

"And I'm telling *you* no," I reply. "But thank you for proving your point from last night. You were right. We can't be personally involved because it's affected how you think."

"I'm protecting you."

"You gave up years of your life trying to take down Waters and every sin he forced on you, every person he hurt, doesn't matter if we stumble now."

"Ending up dead is a pretty fucking big stumble, Pri."

"I get that. I chose to put my life on the line, not like you, but I have, or I wouldn't be in a damn cave. I *cannot, we cannot,* back down now."

"Regrouping is not backing down."

"I need to interview Deleon sooner than later. And I need your input during that process. We have to be a team. We *have* to do this."

He studies me, a muscle in his jaw ticking before he pushes to his feet, his chin lifting, face tilting to the ceiling. I haven't looked at the ceiling, not really and I don't want to know what's up there, because it's likely a bunch of bugs. Besides, I'm looking at him, just him, waiting on a response.

But it doesn't come.

He just keeps looking at the ceiling, clearly tormented about what comes next. I decide to give him space. We're suddenly masters of giving each other space when there's none to give.

I hurry behind the sheet, use the bathroom, and wash up every way possible. That includes putting on my damp bra, but I'm stuck with the giant sweats. My pants are just too filthy and wet. I put on my bra but leave my mud-caked pants where they are.

A loud crash jolts me. Adrenaline surges and I whip around the curtain as Adrian draws his weapon and points it at the cavern entrance.

Chapter Eleven

PRI

A light flashes through the cave entrance and repeats three times. Adrian lowers his weapon at the obvious code, glancing over his broad shoulder at me. "That's our team," he says. "Stay put."

This news delivers about ten seconds of comfort followed by a mental push back.

Stay put?

In a cave?

While he goes and gets killed?

I watch Adrian shrink down and squeeze through the hole and nothing about that feels right, especially the part where I wait for trouble. Darting into action, I retrieve my weapon, the heavy steel a cold comfort in my hand as I stand where I am, near the center of the cavern, ticking off seconds. A full minute becomes two and still, there are no signs of Adrian. Another minute passes and I start to pace. Another minute turns into two more, and I'm officially nervous. The cavern begins to close in on me, prickly energy starting to claim control of me. I decide Adrian's right. The claustrophobia is about the sensation of being trapped. Until now, the cave actually felt safe, a shelter, but now it's a prison. One I can't escape easily, not when I don't know what is going on outside, but what if that wasn't

Walker? Or what if Walker betrayed Adrian? Waters' influence runs deep. Oh God. He might need my help.

That very idea sets me in motion.

With my gun in hand, I charge toward the cavern exit, but just as I'm on my hands and knees, about to crawl out of it, Adrian is crawling inside. And there we are, on hands and knees, facing each other, close, too close for all that is between us. The air crackles, the awareness we share thick like honey that is somehow sticky and bittersweet.

He motions me back inside the cave and I quickly scoot backward and rest on my haunches, nervous all over again. "What's happening?" I ask again, this time urgently.

"Adam and Savage are here," he says, fully entering the cave and before I can steel myself for the impact, he's catching my arm and helping me to my feet. Once again, heat dashes up my arm, across my chest, and the air thickens between us.

As if he realizes what he's done, his hand falls away, but he's still close, so very close, staring down at me. "Grab anything you need. We need to leave."

There's a shuffling behind us and Adrian shifts to stand beside me as Savage hauls his huge body into the small space. "Hello campers," he says, straightening, running big hands over his fatigues. "Are the s'mores toasty and ready for me yet?"

Adam crawls on in as well and in unison, Adrian and I take a step back, offering them space where there isn't much to give. All three men are big, the sheer size of them shrinking the cavern, but still, I don't feel freaked out, or claustrophobic. This isn't triggering me. The fact that they are both wearing camouflage, ready to blend in and fight, isn't either, but it likely should.

"You look like shit," Savage says, giving me a once over.

"Thank you, Savage," I say dryly, but I'm not offended. I have claimed to value honesty and I do.

Adam elbows Savage and tries to smooth things over. "What he means, Pri—"

"Is what he said," I supply. "I do look like shit, but I'm alive. Thanks to Adrian," I say, glancing up at him. "Thank you."

He studies me a few beats and says, "But?"

"I have to interview Deleon," I say, glancing between Savage and Adam. "If he's alive?"

"Of course, he's alive," Adrian snaps. "I didn't kill him, Pri." His voice is utter frustration, pinched with anger.

"I know," I say quickly, turning to face him, hands up. "I know. That was a stupid comment. I meant—I just, I need to interview him."

Savage snorts. "Good luck with that one. He disappeared."

I whirl on him. "What?" I glance around the circle of men. "How is that even possible?"

"Obviously, his people got to him before we did," Adam supplies. "And they focused on clean-up rather than pursuing the two of you."

"Clean-up?" I ask.

"Pitt's gone, too," Adrian supplies. "He took him."

I huddle into myself, my arms folding in front of me with the blow of this news. "He's dead then." My gaze finds Adrian's. "Right?"

"Yes," he says, his jaw set hard. "We can assume he's dead, but that is not your fault."

I face him again. "It's not yours, either."

"Yes," he says. "It is. I let Deleon live, just like I let Waters live."

59

For me, I think. "Then it is my fault," I say. "You did that for me."

"He did it," Adam says, "because it was the right thing to do. That's what we do. The right thing. All of us."

"Except me," Savage says. "But don't tell my wife."

"He won't walk away alive again," Adrian says. "No matter how wrong that might be."

I study the lines of his face, the sharp cut to his features that isn't always present. He studies me right back, his gaze hooded. He told me this isn't my fault, but I think he believes otherwise. He thinks I make him weak. He thinks I'm bad for him.

Maybe we're bad for each other.

Hugging myself again, I face forward again and glance between Adam and Savage. "Now what?" I ask again.

"S'mores?" Savage asks.

In other words, he's not even going to think about answering my question. "Right now," Adrian replies, "we're going to another safe house. Once we're rested and showered, we'll talk about what comes next."

It's not what I expect, it's not a push to leave the city he'd given me earlier, and I can only hope that means I got through to Adrian. Or there's something else I don't know. I'm suddenly hyper-aware of the three giant men sharing a cave with me when Adrian seemed to think they'd wait outside. Adam and Savage took cover for a reason.

I don't need to think hard about that reason. Deleon and his men know we went into the woods. They expect us to come out.

My eyes dash to Adrian's hard, unreadable expression, but the hard edge of a sharper mood screams at me. "Tell me what to do."

A barely perceivable flicker of relief flashes in his eyes, and he says, "Grab what you need. We move now."

I waste no time tearing out the pages of the notebook I'd made use of last night, shoving them in my purse, and it over my shoulder. When I'm done, Savage and Adam are gone and Adrian waits for me at the exit. My belly clenches with the tug of war between us and I close the space between me and him.

Once I'm right in front of him, I expect him to move, to motion me out of the cave, but for long moments, he just stares down at me. There is something he wants to say, something that hangs and cuts and bleeds between us. Finally, when the pulse of tension between us cuts too deep, when I can't take it another moment, he breaks the silence.

"Deleon knows we went into the woods. He won't know if we came out or not. He's also not a fool. He'll be watching. He'll have men waiting."

"I assumed as much," I say, my throat dry, voice raspy.

"Once we're out there, silence is golden," he says. "You stay with me, by my side. Hold onto me if you need to, Pri."

Somehow it feels as if he's talking about more than our escape from the woods, but I don't know. I just don't know right now. "Without hesitation," I say. "I trust you. Remember?"

"Do you?"

"Yes," I insist, but I think of his reaction to me asking if Deleon was dead. He doubts my trust and now isn't the time for that conversation. I know that. "I do."

He doesn't respond but I feel the cut of his attention as he steps away and motions to the exit.

Chapter Twelve

PRI

I exit the cave to find Savage and Adam waiting on us, the sun just piercing the horizon, dampness from the rain now gone, lingering on the ground and in the air. Adrian is quickly by my side, and despite all that is a mixed-up, ripe eruption of confusing emotion between us, there is a comfort to the protectiveness that radiates from him. Every part of me knows that this man would die for me, but I also know he'll walk away from me and hurt me.

Wordlessly, he motions to Savage.

Savage responds by taking the lead position, setting out on a forward march, claiming the conductor role in this little train, though I have a sense that Adrian is in control. As if proving this to be true, Adrian signals to me to follow Savage, but rather than stepping to my rear, he remains by my side. Adam instead claims the tail end of our little train, the man who ensures no one kills us from behind.

The sun inches into view, a dull orange glow, ready to blast us with Texas heat, and plenty of sunlight. It's only now, watching it rise, in our exit formation, that I wonder why we didn't leave under the cover of darkness, but I don't ask questions. Now is not the time for conversation, and I'm confident enough in this group to know they have good reasons. They are the experts at survival, while it's on me to be an expert in the courtroom when I face Waters. And I will, in a few short weeks.

We maneuver down the smooth rocks of the cavern that had been our shelter. Once we reach the clearing that Adrian and I had raced across the night before, Savage halts and holds up a hand.

We pause and wait as he scans our surroundings. My pulse kicks up a beat, with the idea that he might know of a threat we do not. The courtroom, not the forest, is my safe place, the zone where I excel, where I easily spot trouble, but as I visually hunt for it now, I find nothing. He must not either, as he waves us forward. My pulse slows and Adrian captures my hand, the mere act creating the collision of our stares he's clearly intended. He lifts his chin toward the clearing. Savage shoots into action, running forward, and Adrian follows, leading me along with him, through mud and too much open space for comfort. Adrenaline is my friend and enemy, blurring my surroundings, and thus my ability to spy an enemy, but it also leaves me with nothing but a forward movement. Finally, in what is likely only a minute but feels like a year, we're in the forest, and branches and foliage offer the coverage the new day has stolen.

There's no dilly-dallying around either. We're already moving again, our path rugged and filled with obstacles. In the light of day, and the downpour over, snakes are probably less of a problem than flying bullets, but still worthy of creating caution.

But we don't tread cautiously, not at all. We charge onward, one mile that becomes two, I think, mosquitoes and gnats swarming us in suffocating numbers. Still, we press onward. Finally, we cut up a hill and a paved road comes into view, as do three motorcycles. I assume they're our rides home, but then Savage holds up a hand again and starts walking toward the bikes on his own. My heart leaps with the obvious possibility that they belong to the Devils. Adrian somehow reads me and catches my gaze. He mouths, "Ours."

I breathe out, relief expelled from my chest, and already Savage is motioning us forward. Adrian claims a shiny black motorcycle with a yellow streak. He hands me a helmet and I've actually never been on a bike, but not much rattles me. Well, except tunnels under cabins that could collapse at any moment.

Securing my helmet, Adrian does the same of his and throws his leg over the bike. Savage and Adam have already mounted. I don't have to be told to climb on behind Adrian, not when I want the heck out of here. I hike myself on board and wrap my arms around him, and he grabs my hands and closes my fingers around his belt loops.

Once I'm secure, the three men lift hands in the air, seeming to complete some count before, in unison, they rev their engines. Adrian is the first to pull onto the road, but we are not alone. A cluster of three motorcycles blast out of the woods and in our direction. I scream as gunfire rips through the air and Adrian shouts, "Hold on!"

I'm already leaning into Adrian, holding on to his belt now, and it's a good thing. He swerves, left and right, no doubt trying to turn us into a difficult target. Savage and Adam's bikes appear by our sides and both men hold weapons, firing behind us. A motorcycle skids off the road.

Adrian zooms past the scene, accelerating, leaving Adam and Savage to handle our attackers. Our path appears free, but our speed is intense, and at moments, we're all but sideways as we travel wild curves left and right until Adrian directs us off the road. We skid to an abrupt halt and he says nothing, focused on his intent, which appears to be him acting on his fear that I'm not secured properly.

He grabs a rope from I don't know where, and wraps it around us, anchoring me to him before he knots it hard. My heart thunders wildly with the silent promise that we're in for a wicked ride.

Already we're moving again, and my God, it's rough, jolting terrain and my one comfort is that Adrian drives it like a man who knows this ground. His confidence feeds my confidence in his skill and our survival. That is until he sends us flying in the air, over a ditch. I'm screaming into the wind when we land hard and solid on the dirt terrain just off the roadway.

Our landing sends air gushing from my lungs as we blast forward and away from the highway. Slowly the spike of adrenaline calms, and I hug Adrian, expecting the unexpected. I don't know how long I press my cheek to his back and hold on for dear life, but finally, finally, we return to the main, albeit remote, road again and our path is smoother.

What follows are long winding roads until we reach a major highway. Only then does Adrian pull to the edge of a gas station just long enough to flip up his visor and ask, "Are you okay?"

"Yes," I say flipping up my visor, appalled he stopped just because of me, but of course, I did freak out in a hole. "Good. Go. Get us out of here."

And thank God, he does.

In a blink, we're pulling onto the highway again and with trouble seemingly behind us, I worry about how long it's been since we saw Savage and Adam. Please let them be okay. Relief comes hard and fast as our path transforms into the familiar territory of Austin's Hill Country and Cat Mountain neighborhood.

In what I sense is our final trek, Adrian navigates the winding roads. About a mile up the road, he draws to a halt at the gate of a mansion set on top of a hill, with expansive grounds.

The gates open and Adrian maneuvers us down a long tree-covered path and turns us down a circle drive. The house is white stucco with several flights of steps leading to a heavy dungeon-style red door. Never before has the Asian red door for luck been kinder to my eyes. I'll take luck where we can claim it, anywhere we can claim it.

The bike hums to a stop just beyond the front door.

The instant he kills the engine and unties me, I climb off and remove my helmet. Adrian does the same, attaching his to the bike and then doing the same with mine. And then he's facing me, staring down at me—tall, dark, and deadly, and I like it.

"You okay?" he asks.

"Yes," I assure him. "Completely. Amazing driving by the way. You really know how to—"

Suddenly, his hand is on my waist, possessive and warm, his touch stealing my words. He steps into me and I barely have time to catch my breath before his fingers twine in my hair, tilting my mouth to his. He hesitates, his mouth so close to my mouth, that I can almost taste him. I *need* to taste him. And then he's kissing me, a deep, drugging, drag-me-under-his-spell kind of kiss that melts me right here in my shoes.

Engines roar up the driveway and a door opens. Adrian abruptly ends the kiss, releasing me, his chin lowering to his chest, eyes shut, lashes shadowing his cheeks. There's a punch of regret in that action that tells me that kiss changes nothing. We are no more. He was simply riding the mix of adrenaline and all the crazy push and pull of emotions between us.

By the time a tall man with dark hair exits the house and Savage and Adam halt their bikes next to Adrian's, I know our team is safe, at least for now. And I know where I stand with Adrian. At a distance.

Chapter Thirteen

PRI

The man I'd seen exit the house hurries toward us and extends his hand in my direction. "Hi, Pri. I'm Blake Walker."

"Blake," I say shaking his hand. "How are you here? *Why* are you here?" I can feel myself pale, adrenaline spiking again for a whole new reason. "God. Please tell me—"

"They're fine," Adrian says, his hand settling on my back, warm with promise and comfort, and when I look up at him, he confirms, "Your parents are fine."

I breathe out in relief. "Thank you."

"I would have told you if something had happened."

"I know," I say. "I know. I just thought—while we were on that bike—" I turn to Blake. "And you're obviously here for a reason."

"You two were hiding in a damn cave," he says. "How the fuck could I not be here? When one of our own is in trouble, we stand with them." He eyes Adrian. "That means you, asshole." He doesn't give Adrian a chance to reply. He motions to the door. "Let's all go inside and talk and then you two can shower and get some rest."

Savage and Adam join us and Savage grins and adds, "Because you look like shit. Just in case I forgot to tell you."

"You did tell me," I say. "And I know you remember."

He grins. Blake arches a brow at him. "As my mama would say, you're the pot calling the kettle black, man. You look like shit, but then, you were born that way, Savage. You can't wash that off."

I laugh and Adrian and I exchange a look—it just sort of happens, a familiar, intimate look, and yet the strain between us is there, a pulse that refuses to be ignored. Blake leads a path up the stairs, with Savage flanking him and talking smack. They're family, I realize then, brothers. I understand why Adrian defended them so heartily when I suggested one of them might have betrayed him. They're his family and yet so was his brother. I wonder—I wonder so many things.

Adam steps closer, parallel to me and Adrian, and gives me an inspection. I laugh. "Are you going to tell me I look like shit, too?"

"No," he assures me. "I was just going to ask how you are. You had a hell of a ride out there."

"I'm good," I say. "Thank you for asking. It was actually kind of fun." I laugh at the insanity of that reply. "Well, aside from the men shooting at us and the fact that we could have rolled and died at any moment."

He smiles. Adam has a nice smile, a warm smile. A Captain America kind of smile, filled with charm and honor. "There was that." He glances at Adrian. "I'll see you inside."

Adrian gives a barely perceptible nod and Adam walks away. I assume we will follow, actually taking a step to do so, but Adrian halts me with a softly spoken, "Pri."

I pause, aware that he's avoiding touching me. Facing him, our eyes collide, and Lord help me, that pulse is back. It never went away. "Are you really okay?" he asks.

"Yes," I assure him. "You can stop worrying. I'm pretty darn daring as long as you don't shove me into a small space."

The rapidly rising sun beams down on us, almost as if it's a warm spotlight, burning hotter by the moment. He steps closer, the air charging between us. "I know more about small spaces than you might think. And boxes. I'm in one now."

I blink, surprised by this reply when I perhaps shouldn't be. He is a man of secrets who dances with demons. And Waters is only one of them. The worst is the one of his own creation. The one he calls his own self-hatred. "Yes," I agree. "I do believe you are."

He studies me for several heavy seconds, and I hold my breath, waiting for a reply, for more. He doesn't seem to ever give me more.

Blake shouts, "You two coming?!"

For a beat, Adrian ignores him, his attention locked on me, a deep burn in his eyes that fades and then disappears as if a shutter had been dropped. "On our way!" he calls out, turning away from me, and while his energy says he's withdrawn, his hand settles on my back, urging me forward.

And that hand is still possessive.

That's exactly why his touch both scorches me and confuses me, but that comment he just made does not. When he testifies, the defense will demonize him. He and everyone around him will have to live with all those dirty stories, all the dirty pieces of his life. And they will call him a bad man. That's his box. The one where he lives as a bad man for the rest of his life, not the hero he deserves to be called. I decide right then that I'm going to get him out of that box. One way or the other,

we will take down Waters without him destroying
Adrian. For now, I focus on how we stay alive and that
starts with gleaning all the information I can from this
"talk" Blake wants to have.

Chapter Fourteen

PRI

The house turns out to be as gorgeous and elaborate as the exterior and grounds suggest. One of those oh-so-chic Austin places with lots of windows, bountiful views of the hill country, big open spaces, and modern finished concrete floors. Adding to the modern look, glass-encased stairwells lead up and down to additional levels of the house. A giant balcony seems to wrap around the house and overlook a pool. This place is worth at least two million.

"This is quite the safe house," I say, as Adrian and I walk through a living area with navy blue couches and a matching rug.

"It's all about location and size," he says. "On a hilltop, surrounded by neighbors with security footage that complements ours, and a view of whoever is coming from all directions. As a plus, it has plenty of room for all of us."

A large team, I think. That's how complicated and dangerous this case has become. We need a large team. We need a hill to see our enemy approach. Unbidden, I'm back in the cabin, trying to stop Pitt from bleeding out. He's dead. There's no question he's dead and that guts me. It scares me, too, but I'm angrier than I am afraid. I have to win this war. I *will* win this war.

Blake and company are waiting for us in the open-concept kitchen, around a rectangular marble island, with the added headcount of Lucifer. He and Blake have claimed the endcaps and set-up their MacBooks for action.

Adrian and I step to this side of the island and Lucifer eyes me and Adrian and says, "Jumanji level one successfully played. Level two coming right up."

Meanwhile Savage is at the stainless-steel fridge, holding up two beers. "Jackpot."

I'm pretty sure it's about eight in the morning, but I don't comment. At this point, time feels rather irrelevant. I wave off his offer of a bottle of my own, but Adrian does not. He twists off his top and slugs back a drink, comfortable here, unwinding no doubt, while I am still fact-gathering. "Is there any news on Pitt?"

"None," Blake says. "And there won't be. No body, no crime, at least not one easily proven."

"Right," I say flatly. "It's our word against Deleon's, and he plans on us being dead."

"He better pray I die before I get to him again," Adrian murmurs, setting down his beer. "Do we know how Pitt found us?"

"I can help there," Lucifer offers. "He got a text last night that looked like it was from you, Adrian. Looks like a burner phone. I'm in the process of tracking his activity for the past couple of months, to see where that leads us."

Savage steps to the spot across from Adrian. "How did anyone know about that cabin?"

"One of my brothers," Adrian says. "That's the only way anyone could know and I find it hard to believe Raf would tell anyone about this place."

"You have two brothers?" Lucifer asks. "I thought you just had one."

"Alex is dead," Adrian says. "But in life, he talked too much." He offers nothing more. In fact, he moves on. "Is the DA secure?"

"Oh God, yes," I say quickly. "Is Ed secure?" I glance at Savage. "I thought you were going to stay with him?"

Savage sets own his beer. "My boy Ed is with Jacob and Dexter on a plane to New York, and out of Deleon's reach."

"I almost forgot Dexter was involved," I say, thinking of all the manpower involved in fighting this war with Waters.

"After Deleon missed his first targets," Blake adds, "moving Ed feels like a good strategy. If Waters is desperate to end the trial, going after Ed seems like his next move."

"Or the judge," I say. "I can't believe I haven't thought of the judge, though he'd be easier to replace than Ed."

"Not at the holiday on this high-profile a case," Blake argues. "We can't offer the judge protection. It's a conflict of interest, considering he's supposed to be neutral and we're on the side of the prosecution. I did connect him with someone I trust. And the DA did talk to him and stress the importance of seeing the trial through."

"I'd hoped that we could make that easier by flipping Deleon," I say.

Adrian snorts and tips back his beer before he says, "I told you, that was never going to happen. The only good news is he's hurt. He's not going to be the one coming after anyone for a while."

"But he'll send someone else," Blake says. "Who will that be?"

"I can make a list of the top five options," Adrian says, "but the Devils are broad and deep. Waters wants us dead. That means he put a price on our heads. His followers will come from all over to serve Waters via Deleon."

I don't allow myself to think about just how terrifying that concept is. I focus on the case, on the witnesses, on making every sacrifice count. "Please tell me my witnesses are safe," I say.

"They are," Blake assures me. "And we've made sure they feel safe, too. No one else in this group of witnesses is going to back out on you. But that only matters if you and Adrian make it to the trial alive."

I read exactly where this is headed and I rotate to face Adrian. "Even if Blake tells me to go to New York, too, it does not mean I'm going. I get why Ed needed to leave. He's dead, we're dead, but if I die, he can take over. I need to work the case."

"You can," Adrian insists. "Do it remotely."

"I need to meet with the judge and if we manage to capture one of Waters' people, I need to be here to interview that person."

"We can have you back here in a few hours," he argues.

"The first few hours are critical in an interrogation," I counter.

"That's why they have law enforcement," he snaps back.

"Who might be dirty," I argue. "Come on, Adrian. You of all people know how deep the corruption with Waters runs."

He glowers, hands settling on his hips. "You're the most stubborn woman I have ever known."

"And you, Adrian Mack, are the most hardheaded man I've ever known. This isn't about your personal baggage."

"And yet, it is, Pri, in more fucking ways than you know."

"That's because you won't tell me."

"She's right on that," Adam agrees.

"Yep," Savage chimes in.

"They sound married," Lucifer says. "Are they getting married?"

Married?

My God, what is he saying and why is he saying it now?

My cheeks heat and Adrian rotates away from me to face them. "Are you trying to convince her to stay or go, assholes?"

"She should go," Adam says, eyeing me. "You *should* go. If you're dead, it's over. Dead is pretty much the end."

"I need to meet with the judge," I repeat.

"You and the judge need to keep a distance," Adrian snaps. "Teleconference with him."

"If we leave," I say, glancing over at him, my eyes burning, no doubt, "Deleon goes after someone else."

"You're right," Adrian says, facing me again. "Which is why I already decided that I'll stay. Adam will take you to New York City."

My eyes go wide. "So, you're passing me off so you can carry out your death wish alone?" I don't wait for a reply. "No," I say. "No. I'm not leaving. I intend to take Waters down and I can't do that by hiding."

Blake stands up. "I think you both need a shower and some rest. We can talk this out later tonight."

"Yep," Savage says again. "You two are stinky."

"Lower right bedroom," Blake says. "And Pri, I set you up a secure phone and MacBook. We also brought over some of your things."

Adrian scrubs his jaw and settles his hands back on his hips before glancing at me. "He's right. We'll fight later. I need a damn shower."

I nod, but anger tics in my jaw. "Fine. Later, but I'm not giving in." I glance around the room. "Thank you all. I'm fairly certain I'd be too dead to argue about how to get myself killed if it weren't for all of you," I joke.

No one laughs. Instead, Blake says, "You fit right in, Pri. These guys are always volunteering to get themselves killed for the greater good. Fortunately, we always find a way to get the job done and keep everyone alive."

I fit right in.

There is a pinch in my chest, a past pain, and now *my* demons are the ones asking me to dance while they declare permanent residence in my life. Fitting in is exactly what I wanted once upon a time. And then I discovered fitting in can come with a price. With my father, that meant giving up my soul. If fitting in here means giving up someone else's life, then I'm not okay with that.

I start to turn away from the group when Blake says, "Pri."

I glance back at him. "Use your technology as needed," he says, "but full disclosure. I forwarded your calls to that phone. I'm also listening in. You have zero privacy right now."

"Your team signed confidentiality agreements and I have no private life. I can forgo privacy for the greater good. I just want to catch Waters."

"Right there with you," he replies and Savage, Adam, and Lucifer hold up their breakfast beers, and add a cheer of, "Here, here."

I almost smile, but tiredness wears heavy. There is no denying the surge of confidence and unity I feel.

I've often had a team around me, but until Walker, until right now, I still felt as if it was me against the world. This shift to having a team is all because of Adrian. I glance up at him and he motions toward the stairs. We head in that direction and travel to the lower landing, side by side, but without words.

Two flights down we pass through a lower level complete with a fancy full bar, a living area, and a pool table on our way to a hallway, and then a door. Adrian opens it and motions me forward. I step inside the massive, master bedroom with its own bathroom, and expect him to follow, but he does not. He lingers in the doorway.

I turn to face him, expectancy in the action.

Instead, I get his command. "Rest. It's been a hell of a ride."

"You're not staying?"

"I don't think that's a good idea. And I want to check on my brother before I lay down."

His rejection punches me in the chest and I hug myself, fighting the impact. "All right," I say, "but I wanted to tell you that I was wrong to question Walker. I know they didn't betray us. I'm not used to having people I can trust around me. I'm lucky to have them working on this and I know that's because of you."

He draws a barely perceptible breath and then says, "You're still trying to make this about trust. You still don't understand."

I step toward him. "Adrian—"

"Rest, Pri. We both need rest." He backs up, shuts the door, and then he's gone.

Chapter Fifteen

ADRIAN

I head upstairs, where I hunt down my bag that thankfully hasn't been put in with Pri's stuff, and just when I think I've escaped a conversation, I hear my name.

Grimacing, bag on my shoulder, I walk into the kitchen where Blake is sitting at the kitchen island. "Shower and sleep, then conversation," I say, "unless you have a location where I can go kill Deleon."

"I do not," he says.

"Sleep it is," I say. "Where's my room?"

"With Pri, asshole," Savage says, "Make up with her before you screw that shit up."

I grimace and start to turn away but stop myself. "Rafael? Anything from the team watching him?"

"He's good, man." He glances at his watch. "He's in Paris, right about now, on stage, performing."

Thank fuck, I think.

With a nod of appreciation, I turn away, jogging back down the stairs. Me and my bag end up in the downstairs bedroom, where I find a duffle on the bed. I don't know who's claimed this room and I don't care. It has its own bathroom, which I'm about to claim.

Tossing my bag on the tiled bathroom floor, I strip down. The lure of the hot water is real and I step under the showerhead, and soap up, washing away the weather and the forest, but I can't wash away my sins or my mistakes that keep piling up. I press my hands on the tiled surface of the shower, chin to my chest, those sins, and bad decisions eating me alive. My inability to stay the fuck away from Pri is eating me alive right along with them.

The door to the bedroom opens, and my first thought is Pri. She's looking for me. Adrenaline drives away my weariness and I turn off the shower, yank the towel from above and wrap it around my waist. Opening the door, I step out of the shower to find Savage leaning on the doorframe between the bathroom and the bedroom. He wiggles an eyebrow. "I had no idea you liked me like this, Adrian."

I ignore him. That's the best way to handle Savage's humor, that or a stupid joke of my own, and I *really* don't have one in me. "What do you want, Savage?"

"What happened to you and the sexy ADA?"

"Nothing I plan to tell you. I barely like you."

"You love me and you know it. Talk."

"I'm wearing nothing but a towel, Savage."

"And I have all the same manly parts as you but better." His tone shifts and darkens. "What the fuck is your deal?"

The bedroom door opens again and Savage swings his big body into the bedroom. "We have our Adam," Savage says, poking his head back into the bathroom. "He still has no Eve."

Rolling my eyes, I murmur, "Lord help me," and reach for the clothes I set out before I got in the shower.

"Is he here?" Adam demands.

"Yes," I call out, already pulling on my pants. "He is here." I walk into the bedroom to find Adam hovering at the door. "Are we having a Walker family reunion?" I eye Adam. "Or do we have real news on Deleon?"

"We do not," Adam says. "But something went wrong with our plan. "

"Yeah," Savage says. "Let's talk about what went wrong. Who knew about the cabin?"

"I told you," I say. "My family."

"Right," Savage says. "Is Rafael fucking you over?"

My teeth grind together. "Rafael is not fucking me over. Alex—"

"Is dead," Savage supplies. "Dead people don't dance, sing, or fuck people over."

I scrub a hand through my damp hair, too damn tired to be dragged down this rabbit hole. "Alex and I were both undercover inside the Devils."

Savage's eyes go wide. "No shit. How did I not know that?"

Adam studies me long and hard. "I didn't know either."

"I thought it was irrelevant," I reply. "As you said, Savage, he's dead."

The door opens and fucking Lucifer walks in. "Donuts in the kitchen. Six dozen. Almost enough to go around, so grab 'em and run."

"This," I say, "would be a good time for everyone but me to go eat the damn donuts."

Blake appears in the doorway and it's official. Everyone in the house who isn't Pri is here. Blake's brown, intelligent eyes meet mine and I don't know what he finds in my stare, but his chin lifts slightly before he says, "Everyone who isn't Adrian should go eat the fucking donuts." He steps further in the room, a charge in the air around him, a sense of power and control, and no one questions it or him. No one argues. They leave.

Blake shuts the door. Exhaustion weighs on my shoulders and back and I sit down on the end of the bed. He steps in front of me and leans on the dresser. "What happened out there?"

I don't ask what "out there" means. He's talking about the shit show that was my plan to hide out in a secret cabin that wasn't secret at all. A plan that cost at least one man his life.

There are ten reasons I'd like to avoid a direct answer, but none of them allow Blake the chance to go into the rest of this mission with eyes wide open. "I suspect it started with my parents' murder."

"Not what I expected to hear, but somehow, this all makes more sense. I'm going to gamble and say Waters was somehow involved."

"On the surface, it could have been tied to any one of my father's many arrests, but I kept digging. Apparently, Alex did as well. By the time I found the connection to Waters, he was already undercover with the Devils."

"He was on a revenge mission."

"Yes. He was, and if you knew my brother, his form of revenge was leading him nowhere safe." I give a laugh that is all bitterness and add, "I joined the task force with the intent of saving his life."

"And now he's dead."

"Yes. Now he's dead. Alex did just what I knew he'd do. He got in too deep. He was pulled under, seduced by the lifestyle, and I couldn't snap him out of it. I couldn't bring him back."

"It happens to a lot of good men."

"Yeah well, I knew he had a dark side. *I knew*. I never believed he belonged inside the agency, but who was I to make that call?" I glance skyward, fighting a memory of our final fight before I refocus on Blake. "The cabin was always our secret, our safe house if anything went wrong. Obviously, Alex told someone about the cabin."

He's back to studying me a little too hard. "I read you and your brother's files. He disappeared a year after you both went under."

My jaw clenches. I do not like where this is going. "That's right," I agree.

"What aren't you telling me?"

It's a moment of truth, one I owe Blake Walker for all he's done for me. "He's dead. That's all I have to say on that topic."

"I read between the lines and assumed as much. I see you and understand you. What you need to remember is that what we do undercover is different than what we do outside that cover."

"Where are you going with this, Blake?"

"Once upon a time, I wanted vengeance and by vengeance, I mean blood. Then I met Kara. She pulled me back, kept me from becoming something that would have changed me forever. You think you should have killed Deleon. You're wrong."

My lips press together. "He'll kill again. He'll come after Pri, damn it."

"And we'll get him," he replies. "We'll use him. We'll make him talk."

"He won't talk."

"You might be surprised."

"I *won't* be surprised."

"You did the right thing, Adrian. And if you question yourself, if you think you aren't the man you once were, you're wrong. That decision to spare him proves you wrong on that."

"I did it for Pri."

"Pri proved you wrong." He straightens. "Get some rest. You might have a different mindset after a few hours rest."

"I won't."

He ignores that reply and saunters to the door, pausing to glance back at me. "Talk to me before you make any confessions."

"I've asked for a full immunity agreement."

"The trial will be on national television. Nothing gives you immunity from the court of public opinion. In today's world, that alone ruins lives. Let me help you prep." He doesn't leave the topic up for discussion.

He opens the door and leaves the room.

I stand up and run my hand through my damp hair. I don't know what he thinks he knows about anything I've done, but considering this is Blake we're talking about, he probably knows too much. At this point, I'm jittery, raw energy charging my body, and way too much junk is punishing my mind. I'm not sure if I need to take a jog or go to sleep. With both as options, I pull on a T-shirt and by the time I get to my shoes, sleep is already winning. I opt for my boots and grab my bag on my way to the door. I'm *not* sleeping with Savage.

Once I'm in the hallway, the tug of the room where Pri is likely snuggling under nice, cool sheets in a barely-there gown, is real, but I do not cave to temptation. I *do* need rest and so does she and we are a whole lot better at fighting and fucking than we are at sleeping together. And maybe Blake is right. I don't know where my head will be after I sleep.

I end up choosing the theater room for my makeshift bedroom, simply because it's an easy space to create pitch dark during the day. It also has a couch in front of the rows of theater seating. I drop my bag on the floor, lie down on the cushions, and set my weapon on the floor within easy reach.

I shut my eyes and for a moment, I've returned to the cave, Pri naked in my arms, and it's bittersweet. Her smell, her taste, her soft little sounds. *Her trust.* The trust is what grinds through me and I'm instantly transported further back in time, much further back in time. Back to the day that predicted the future.

It was a holiday weekend, and me, Rafael, and Alex had been at the cabin, practicing our marksmanship. I'd been eighteen, about to start college, and Rafael had been only twelve. Alex had been twenty-four, about to enter the FBI training academy. He'd been the big brother we looked up to, despite too many times, that we'd feared him.

But I was getting my legs underneath me, recruiting early for the FBI. I'd felt confident. I didn't fear him anymore and he didn't like it.

I shove aside the memory that will not let me sleep, but I know that that was the day that told a story of one brother killing another.

LISA RENEE JONES

Chapter Sixteen

PRI

My shower is long, and hot, in a fancy bathroom with shiny white tiles and marble floors. My bathroom is stocked with all my products from home, and the closet is filled with two large suitcases packed with my things. I don't dwell on the fact that one of these big alpha men packed for me or the fact that they clearly don't expect me to go home soon. If I dwell on those things, it will take me no place good. I can't focus on my job. But the truth is, once I'm dressed in leggings, a pink tank, and sneakers, clothes I can work or sleep in, the room is too big and too empty.

I stand in the doorway between the bathroom and the bedroom and I'm alone. I feel alone, uncomfortably alone. And it's not because I have trouble being alone. I live alone. I've been on my own most of my life, even when I was working with family and wearing Logan's ring. It's also not because I'm in a strange house, in a giant master bedroom, complete with a king-sized bed. Or the fact that I'm here to hide from an assassin. I knew the dangers of taking this case. No. I'm uncomfortably alone because Adrian is not here.

It feels bad to be without him.

Briefly, I wonder if that's how people feel when they meet the person they fall in love with as if they are better when they are with them than without. I've never felt that way with another human being, but I do now. I dismiss the crazy thought and decide watching Pitt die in a pool of blood is messing with me. I'm feeling dependent on Adrian when I'm not a dependent person. Maybe he sees that in me. Maybe that's why he pulled away. We're not good for each other right now. We're feeding each other's weaknesses. Maybe, maybe he should have killed Deleon because if he hurts someone else, I'll know Adrian could have kept it from happening. I will feel to blame.

I give myself a mental shake and walk toward the desk against the wall, obviously set up for my use. Murder is never the answer. That goes against all I stand for as an emissary of the court and our legal system. And I'm *not* falling in love with Adrian, but I do owe him an immunity agreement for what I believe will include murder.

Settling into a cushy rolling chair, I open up the MacBook, and I'm eager to call my boss, but I hesitate. Ed is in Walker's protective custody now. I assume we can communicate, but I decide to be cautious and confirm that's true. I pick up my new phone and my first instinct is to call Adrian, but I stop myself again. He's not here for a reason. He needed a break and some rest. He's probably smarter than me and sleeping. Alone. In another bedroom. My teeth grit and I dial Blake's number. "Pri," he answers. "Shouldn't you be sleeping?"

"I will," I say, the weariness in my body a dull ache that I can ignore for only so long. "Believe it or not, I slept a little in the cave. I just need to handle a couple of things. Can I call Ed right now?"

"He's still traveling," he says. "He's presently in the air on his way to New York City. How important is it?"

"Important but not life-threatening. I owe some paperwork to a witness. I don't want to let him down."

He hesitates a moment and then he says, "I see. Once he lands, we'll get him on a secure line. That's going to be a while. You should sleep."

"Right. I know. Can I email Ed the document and he'll be able to get it?"

"Yes. I'll let him know to check his email ASAP."

"Great. And can I return my calls and operate as usual?"

"You can. Yes."

"And if people ask where I am?"

"Working remotely. At home, if you're forced to give a location."

"And my parents?"

"Still the same. We have eyes on them. We'll talk about where all of this goes when you and Adrian are rested."

"Thanks, Blake." I hesitate. "Blake—"

"He's in the theater room sleeping."

In the theater room. Not even in a bed. Anywhere but with me. "Thanks," I say, and when I would disconnect, he says, "You both just need rest. You'll be surprised how that will change things."

"Right. Yes. Okay." I disconnect and press my hands to my face. I quickly draw up the agreement, email it to Ed, and scan my emails, which are overflowing. I don't answer them. I just don't have the energy.

I'm eager to check my phone messages but hesitate. I find an iPhone laying on the desk and plugged in to the wall. I check my messages. I have ten. One is from Grace. "Where are you? I'm worried. I called you four times. I'm going to have Josh use whatever resources he has to find you if you don't call me back soon."

91

"Fabulous," I murmur. I love her, but she now has a boyfriend in private security that is going to get us both killed.

I text her a quick note: *Thanks for worrying. I'm off-site in meetings. All is well. Call you later.*

The next message is from Cindy. "What is going on? Why are you and Ed, and even Ed's secretary MIA? Should I be scared right now? Please call me."

I press my fingers to my temple. I don't even know what to say to her besides, yes, probably, and that's not a good way to handle this. For now, I text Grace: *Can you tell Cindy all is well too, please?*

Her reply: *You're sure you're fine?*

Better if I had chocolate right about now, I say, *but yes. All is well. Gotta run.*

Thankfully she accepts that answer, and I finish going through messages, scribbling notes as I listen to mostly work-related content from that point onward. Then there is the final message, from Logan. "We need to talk. In person. It's urgent. Call me."

He's connected to my case, protecting Waters even, I fear. My gut says I should talk to him, but then again— my brow furrows and there's a pinch in my chest. Would he set me up and lure me out and into Deleon's reach? Would a man I was engaged to, who was supposed to be my husband, do such a thing? I can't ignore that call but I'm not sure what to do about it. I'm not even going to try to figure it out right now. I need sleep. I know I need sleep and my mind will be clear on a lot of things. Maybe even Adrian.

Tiredness sweeps through my body, and I leave behind my work and curl up on top of the bed. I set my alarm for two hours, which will still have me up before noon. The minute my eyes shut, I'm back on that cavern mattress, naked with Adrian's mouth on my body. But then the images shift and I'm back in time, back to a moment when I was still engaged to Logan.

Suddenly, I'm drifting back to the last holiday party for my father's firm that I attended as a member of the staff, inside a private mansion rental. *The mansion is decorated with at least a half dozen trees, while fancy lights seem to flicker in unison with the nearby violin player. The crowd is large, mingling here on the lower level, as well on a wraparound porch and outdoor area, complete with a dance floor. The guests, who've traveled in from all over the country, are dressed in fancy gowns and tuxedos. As for me, Logan did the whole Pretty Woman routine and had my gown delivered to my house, a far too expensive, emerald green floor-length gown, with a tasteful slit and a square bodice.*

"What's going on with Logan?" my mother asks, catching up with me on the porch, on my way to the outdoor area. She looks seasonally lovely in a red dress with just a hint of sparkle. I wonder if Dad chose it. That's the thing about the men in our world. No matter how strong we might be, they like their hands in everything, even our attire.

Tonight, it's stifling. Often lately it's stifling.

My brows dip. "I'm not sure what you mean?"

"He and your father were off to the side of the house, and I do believe I heard shouting."

"The golden boy and Dad? Really?"

She nods. "And tonight, of all nights. They both avoid scandal like the plague."

"Can you try to find out what's going on?" I ask.

"Of course, I'll try, but I think you might have a better shot with Logan."

I snort. "They're two of a kind, Mom. I'm not sure why either of us put up with it."

She tilts her head. "Oh no. What's that about?"

I wave her off. "Nothing for tonight. Where is he now?"

"I'm not sure."

"I'll go get him a glass of that expensive whiskey he likes and hunt him down. Never fear, Mother, I'll try to get the answers we both know we'll never know."

"You're not yourself tonight."

At just the right moment, one of my mother's girlfriends appears by her side. I embrace the opportunity to escape inside. I head to the second level of the mansion where a VIP bar is set up. At present no one is in line, and the guests are mingling around expensive leather furniture. I'm about to order Logan's whiskey, when he's suddenly by my side, catching my hand.

"Come with me."

He's already walking, tugging me along with him, and I'm grimacing. The man is proving my point about being controlling. He heads down a hallway and enters a doorway. To my disbelief, I'm pulled inside a tiny bathroom, so small there is no tub. He shuts the door and locks it, and then I'm against the wall and his hands are all over me.

"What are you doing, Logan?" I shove on his chest. "We aren't—"

He kisses me and I bite his lip. He growls. "What the fuck, Pri? How about being here for me?"

"I'm not doing this now. You know I don't like small spaces. I'm suffocating."

"Once I'm inside you, you won't be thinking about small fucking places."

He turns me to the sink and yanks up my skirt. "Stop it, Logan." I try to move but his legs are holding *my legs, and I think I'm starting to feel that trigger I get. I'm panicking.* "Stop."

"Your father pissed me off, baby. If I don't let off the energy, I'm going to end up fired." *He rips away my panties and then he's inside me. The room is hot and I'm struggling to catch a full breath. He's pounding at me, grunting, thrusting. It just won't end. The room spins and I barely know when he shudders and groans.*

His cellphone rings, and he pulls out, dampness clinging to my thighs. I don't turn around. I draw in a deep breath and force myself to calm down. I will not hit him. I will not scream at him. Not here.

"What the fuck is going on?" *he demands into his phone, skipping the hello, or I've just missed it.*

Logan laughs. "You really are a devil. Fuck yeah, you are. I love it. Right. I won't forget this." *He must end the call because he physically moves me out of the way of the door.* "I figured out how to calm your father down. Gotta run, baby." *He turns away from me and exits the bathroom.*

Some part of me must come awake, but I can't quite escape the hell of the past. Suddenly I spiral back into darkness, and when clarity comes, I'm falling. *I land hard at the bottom of a hole, and the pain in my arm and leg is sharp and unbearable. I start to scream.*

LISA RENEE JONES

Chapter Seventeen

PRI

For a moment there is only darkness, inky black darkness. Awareness comes to me with my own screams, and I gasp and sit up straight. In desperation, I scan the room, confirming I am no longer in a deep, suffocating hole. I'm in a room, with Adrian standing at the door with a gun in his hand.

Oh God.

I shift to my knees. "What's happening? Are we being attacked?"

"You were screaming."

I blink. "Screaming?"

"Yes, Pri. Holy hell, woman. You were screaming."

Embarrassment punches at me and I scramble off of the bed. "I'm sorry. Nightmare. God." I hold up my hands. "I'm sorry. I thought I screamed in the nightmare, not out loud."

He runs a rough hand through his dark hair and harnesses his weapon. "You scared the fuck out of me. You know that, right?"

Adam appears in the doorway, looking like Mr. America in his green army fatigues, his weapon in hand. "What the hell is going on?"

"Nightmare," I say. "Sorry, Adam."

"Nightmare," he repeats.

"Yes," I confirm. "Just a nightmare."

"Must have been a hell of a nightmare," he murmurs, harnessing his weapon, too.

"Pink killer bunnies," Adrian supplies, eyeing Adam. "They scare the shit out of her. I found that out the hard way."

Despite Adrian's efforts at deflection on my behalf, I find myself folding my arms in front of my chest, huddling into my embarrassment. Still, I manage to fall right into the silly joke. "The nightmares started when my grandma got me pink bunny slippers as a kid."

Adam looks between us and says, "You've both spent too much time around Savage and his wackadoodle sense of humor, which for the record, is not funny." He glances at Adrian. "I'll leave you to this." He gives me a nod and then disappears into the hallway.

And just that easily, I'm all alone with Adrian, in a bedroom, with, of course, a bed. "Sorry again," I say awkwardly. "Pink killer bunnies really do get to me."

He steps closer, a lot closer, so close that a mere foot separates us, and the freshly showered, spicy scent of him teases my nostrils and stirs heat in my belly. That is until he says, "What was the nightmare about, Pri?"

"Does it matter?"

He studies me a long, probing moment, his expression unreadable before he presses me again. "What was it about?"

"You know what it was about." My brows dip. "But—actually, it didn't start with me in a hole." I tilt my head and think a moment as a realization comes to me. "Logan was in it."

"Logan," Adrian says, and while his tone is flat, there is this sharp disapproving energy about him.

I bristle defensively with that energy, my spine stiffening. "Not in a good way, Adrian. In fact, it was hellish and it was a real memory, and something you don't know about, nor do I feel inclined to share right now."

There's a knock on the door and Adrian grimaces. "Who is it?"

"Adam." He opens the door and peeks in. "A truckload of Chick-fil-A just arrived, Blake's way of getting our asses upstairs and back to work."

"Just the mention of Chick-fil-A makes my stomach growl," I say, eager to escape this fight with Adrian. "I'm in."

Not so eager to do the same, Adrian says. "We'll be right there," without looking at Adam.

The door shuts and I turn, intending to go to the bathroom. Adrian catches my arm, fire shooting from his touch across my shoulder and chest, which only serves to anger me. "Why are you always trying to stop me from going to the bathroom?" I demand. "And I need to eat. I can't remember the last thing I actually did eat. "

His jaw flexes and he hesitates. But he releases me. I don't wait around for him to change his mind about allowing my escape, either. I hurry into the bathroom and shut the door, leaning against it. What is happening with me and this man? Why are we always a tug of war, push, and pull?

I think of the Logan memory and instead of dwelling on how horrible Logan was, how abusive, something about Adrian stands out. He let me go when I demanded he let me go. Logan didn't. He wouldn't. There was more to that memory, but I can't quite put a finger on what. The entire nightmare is a big fuzzy mess.

I push off the door, use the bathroom, wash up and freshen up, including adding a bit of lipstick to my pale lips, and then I open the door. Adrian is leaning on the wall by the door, and he holds up my phone. "Logan called."

I snatch my phone. "Because he's an asshole who wants to use me. I need food." I start walking.

He straightens, catches the fingers of my hand—just the fingers—I think he feels that's less of a bullying act, and it actually is. He steps around and into me, close, so close again, all those manly smells working me over again, his height towering over me. "We need to talk," he says softly.

"You mean fight."

"I don't want to fight with you."

"But we *will* fight. We're very good at fighting. I need food, Adrian," I say. "If we fight right now, while I'm this hungry, you will surely lose. So, you decide. Fight now, or after I eat my Chick-fil-A sandwich?"

He gives me a heavy-lidded stare and then says, "We're not done." And then he releases me, leaving me wondering if he's talking about the topic of Logan, or us. But I don't dare ask or push for answers. I do need food. And I need a few minutes to think about what that memory meant. Because it wasn't about me being fucked in a bathroom while having a panic attack that my fiancé was too arrogant and self-absorbed to realize I was having. That night was a conglomeration of pieces of our relationship that were dysfunctional, and always leading to a split.

Or even the fact that had I been in that bathroom with Adrian, I wouldn't have resisted. Not even a little. It wasn't even about Logan's call and the "devil" remark. It's about the fact that Logan was upset because my father was upset. Whatever the "devil" said on that phone call made Logan happy. That means he felt it would make my father happy.

This case hits a lot closer to home than I could ever have imagined and now I have to decide what to do about it. I want to call my father and confront him, but I know that's a bad idea. I have to make everyone in this house, Adrian included, all of whom are trying to protect me and my family, understand how dirty the foundation on which I stand is.

LISA RENEE JONES

Chapter Eighteen

ADRIAN

I have questions for Pri and things I need to say to her, but I give her the space she's demanded. It kills me, but I do it. I fall back. I fall into step with her on one flight up and bite back a million questions. Like what the fuck did Logan do to give her nightmares?

Fuck.

I can't hold back.

"Pri," I say softly, resisting the urge to capture her hand. "Wait."

We're between the first level and the second when she pauses and turns to face me. Her eyes are so damn blue, and she's so damn beautiful.

I step closer to her and say what's most important right now. "I'm sorry."

She blinks. "What?"

"I'm sorry. I was an ass in the cave. I was an ass in the room back there, too."

Surprise flickers across her face but she quickly says, "I'm sorry, too. And for the record, I'm not sure any man in my life has ever actually apologized. Apology appreciated and accepted."

"I'll try not to be an ass anymore."

She smiles. "You'll try?"

"I prefer to make promises I can keep. Monsters put me in a bad mood, which brings me to Logan."

"Adrian—"

"Did he hurt you?" I ask.

"Why are you asking this now?"

"I just need to know if he's on the list of people I need to kill before I die."

Her lips quirk. "Isn't that a little extreme?"

"I don't know," I answer honestly. "Is it?"

"Yes, but I'm, ah, I' m glad to have someone who cares."

"I do care, Pri." I catch her hand and immediately let it go. "Fuck. Sorry."

Her lips curve and she tangles her fingers with mine. Her hand is tiny and soft, and yet, holding it feels so damn big. "I like it when you touch me," she says, "but we were fighting, and right after that particular nightmare, I needed just a minute to breathe."

"You two coming?"

At the sound of Blake's voice, I glance up to find him leaning over the railing. "Yeah, boss," I say. "On our way." He disappears and I stroke a lock of hair behind Pri's ear. "He might have news. We better go up."

She nods and I lean in, my mouth lingering over her mouth. She presses on my chest, just a tiny bit, enough to get my attention. "I thought we were bad?"

"I have things I'll say about that later, and I suspect you do, too."

"I do," she says. "

"For now, how about I just say this? I'm bad. *We* are not."

"If I'm bad, and you're bad, can we just be bad together?"

I laugh despite myself. "What happened to dirty?"

"Dirty together?" she asks.

"Why, oh why, do you always tempt me so well, Pri?" I kiss her, a low press of tongue to tongue, and her arms wrap my neck, her body softening into mine. I drink her way too long, but not long enough, and then I whisper, "Let's go upstairs before Savage eats all the Chick-fil-A."

She pulls back. "That's actually a real concern. I'm starving."

I laugh. She's the only woman who has ever taken me on a full ride of emotions in a lifetime, let alone a few hours. She's also already darting up the stairs and pulling me along. It feels good to be back on the right side of the law *and* Pri. Maybe I've been wrong about staying away from her because I'm bad. Maybe the very fact that I want and need her is all about me wanting to be on the right side, too. Me wanting to be good.

Maybe I can be saved.

I just hope like hell it doesn't come with a price she pays.

Chapter Nineteen

ADRIAN

Food is taken seriously with the Walker clan. It comes before conversation. With that in mind, it doesn't take Pri and me long to claim our side-by-side seats at the double-sized kitchen island, with Blake and Lucifer at their respective endcaps and Adam and Savage across from us. Nor does it take long for us to start stuffing our faces.

"My God," Pri says, taking a bite of her breaded chicken sandwich. "I love this place. Actually, I just love food in general right now."

I grab a fry and dip it in ketchup. "There was a family of tomatoes—"

"No," Savage and Adam say at the same time as Savage adds, "Do not tell that same stupid-ass ketchup joke again. Get a new one."

"Now I have to hear it," Pri says, smiling at me. She has a beautiful smile worthy of every joke in my arsenal. "Tell the stupid ketchup joke," she encourages. "Do it."

"There was a family of tomatoes," I say. "A mama, a papa, and four kids."

Savage groans. "I've heard this a hundred times. Every client he's ever taken care of has heard this joke."

I ignore him and keep going. "The baby tomato falls behind and the mama is angry. She hurries to the rear and confronts her baby. 'Ketchup!'"

Pri laughs, a sweet, almost luxurious laugh. "That's cute."

Blake snorts. "Cute. See, Adrian? You're all kinds of fucking cute."

"The joke, asshole," I say.

"I'm pretty sure she meant you," Adam agrees. "Cutie pie."

Pri laughs. "I'm just going to eat my sandwich, though you're all pretty cute."

Savage wiggles his eyebrows. "I am, aren't I?"

The conversation stays light, but as the food disappears, Blake turns the conversation to business. Because that's how we work. Eat. Laugh. Work. Repeat. "Pri," he begins. "My brother Royce's wife, Lauren, is an ex-ADA. She's in private practice now. She's offered her services to you free of charge. She's eager to meet you when you get to New York."

And there it is.

The breaking of the ice that will soon become a bomb.

Pri throws her wrapper in a bag. "Thank you and her, Blake," she says primly, the prim is the part that tells me the explosion is imminent. "That's generous," she adds. "and I have no doubt your resources outperform most others. And I know you all want me to be safe." She looks at me. "I get why, too, I do, and part of me welcomes the idea of safety, which I also have no doubt, I'd have there."

"But?" I say, inviting her to say her piece, which is a new strategy. The old dragging her to safety if needed didn't go over well.

"But," she adds, "if Deleon isn't coming for me and you, he's coming for someone else, anyone that might disrupt the trial. And I have you and you have all these resources."

"I know what you think is going to happen," I say, and she turns to look at me. "You want to lure Deleon out again."

"What is wrong with that?"

"If last night proved anything, it's that Deleon is not stupid. He will always be a step ahead of us if we give him the chance." I lean in closer to her. "I hurt him badly, Pri. He'll burrow underground, he'll heal. He'll send soldiers, Devil soldiers, one after another, to kill us."

"Who will go after my staff and the people I love. I can't ask all of them to stand in bullseye formation while I hide."

"You're right," I say. "They will, but not if I'm present and standing in bullseye formation."

"You need me," she says.

I ignore the audience and answer her honestly. "I think I've made that pretty clear. Which is why I need you to go to New York."

"Logan called me." She glances over her shoulder at Blake. "I'm sure you heard."

"I did," he says. "And for the record, he's shady as shit."

"I know," Pri agrees, glancing at me. "The nightmare. I remembered something. The last company Christmas party I attended, Logan and I were still together. He was fighting with my father, which didn't happen. He's the golden child, the son my father never had. Then Logan got a call. His mood shifted. He said, 'you really are a devil' before he hung up. And then he made amends with my father."

"You think Logan has a more direct connection to Waters," Adam assumes.

"Yes," Pri agrees, and then she looks at me. "I'm worried he has one with my father."

"I haven't found one," Blake interjects.

"No," Lucifer agrees. "I've been working heavily on a link between Logan and Waters, looking for a pipeline. There isn't one."

"That doesn't mean it doesn't exist," Pri says. "Throwaway phones. Right? Secret emails. Messengers." She glances at me. "Cabins in names that aren't your own."

Blake's gaze meets mine. "If this were true, how will Waters use this against her?"

I don't have to think about my answer. I know Waters too well. "It depends on how well her father protected himself," I say. "If he has leverage to control Waters, a secret for instance he protects, Waters might consider him off-limits. It might even offer Pri a level of protection she might not otherwise have."

"And if he doesn't?" Pri asks.

"Again, it depends. If your father is deeply seeded with a fair number of his allies, people he needs to protect, he still might hesitate to take him down. However, if it comes to D-day, and that's what it takes to delay the trial to discredit you by connection to your father, he'll do it."

She presses her hands to her face and then looks at me again. "I find it hard to believe that my father is involved. They're trying to kill me. I know he's a bastard, but I don't believe he wants me dead." She stands up. "I know I could be blinded by who he is but—"

"There's no evidence that's he's attached to this," Blake repeats.

"What about Logan?" I ask, trying to get her the answers she looking for, answers that won't cut her and make her bleed. "You said he's shady."

"Shady as fuck, that fucker," Savage mumbles. "He's one I'd enjoy hurting."

"I claim that job," I say, eyeing Blake. "What about him? What about Logan?"

Blake points at Lucifer and Lucifer answers with, "He has three clients with connections to Waters. I haven't found any banking information or electronic connections to Waters, but it doesn't take even a smart person to see it's possible."

She turns fully to me. "Waters could use Logan to ruin my father, and end this trial, correct? He could make it seem like my father's involved?"

"It's possible," I say, catching her hand. "But if I'm a big enough target, they'll focus on me."

"And the problem with that is—" She swallows hard and seems to think twice about what she's about to say. She looks at me. "Can we talk outside, please?"

"Of course," I say, aware that we're about to go to war again. She's right. We're good at fighting, but then, I'm fighting for her life. I've lost too many people. I'm not losing her. And that's exactly what I'm going to tell her.

LISA RENEE JONES

Chapter Twenty

ADRIAN

I open the sliding glass doors and allow Pri to exit to the outdoor space that darn near wraps the house. I'm directly behind her, shutting out our audience. The day is a cooler Texas seventy-something, the scent of rain still a kiss in the light breeze. The clouds once again are a dark, turbulent smoky gray. Pri walks toward the railing, giving me her back, hands on the railing, miles of hill country along the horizon, while the horseshoe-shaped pool is directly below.

I'm on her heels, right there with her, and when she turns to face me, she says, "The problem with that," she says again. "The problem with you making yourself a bullseye is that I don't want you to die." Her voice cracks with emotion. "You don't get to make me need you this much, and then go off and get yourself killed. You don't get to do that."

The emotion radiating from her punches me in the chest. I capture her waist and step into her. "I'm not going anywhere," I say, my voice low, rough, affected. Everything about this woman affects me. "I have too many reasons to live now. You, Pri. You're all of those reasons."

"You can't say that. You can't make yourself a target for Waters and not think you can defy death. We need a plan that keeps everyone alive. I need to meet with Logan."

"No. Absolutely not."

"If he's with them, with Waters and the Devils— and, Adrian, in my gut I know he is—I'll offer him immunity for helping."

"You can't trust him."

"I don't plan on trusting him. I plan to force his hand. My father defends criminals, but I've always known him to walk within the law. He's fine with manipulating the law to the farthest reach for the worst of people, but he won't step outside it. I know Logan broke his rules. I know my father won't appreciate that."

My lips press together, and I go to a place I know she doesn't want to go, but I also need her to see beyond the moment. "He was okay with him fucking his secretary while he was engaged to you."

She barely blinks. "The whole 'men will be men' thing does not screw with my father's finances. This does. This could destroy him."

"He's your father's golden boy, sweetheart. You don't know where that leads." I cup her face and tilt her mouth to mine, lowering my voice. "Let's go to the bedroom and talk."

"We won't talk in the bedroom," she objects weakly, sounding breathless. I like her breathless.

"We need a break."

"We need this to be over."

"But not us, Pri," I say. "Not us."

Her fingers curl on my T-shirt. "What happened to the imminent ending where I hate you?"

"I'm going to take every moment you give me," I say and so I do. I take. My mouth closes down over hers, and I kiss her, drinking her in, tasting her, letting her taste the truth on my tongue. I'm not letting her go. Our lips part and I say those exact words. "I'm falling in love with you, Pri. I'm not letting you go. Not unless you make me."

"You're—you're—"

"Yes. I am."

The door behind us opens and I turn to find Adam standing in the doorway. "Blake needs to see you, Adrian. Now."

His tone is clipped, pure steel. The kind of tone he speaks during high-stress combat situations. Pri catches on, too. "What happened?" she asks urgently, twisting out of my arms. "What's going on?"

He glances at her and then me. "Just come inside."

I draw in a breath and Pri is already storming toward the house. I follow quickly, dread twisting in my gut. Whatever this is isn't good, which is exactly why I catch Pri's hand and give a small tug, halting her, ready to prepare her for the worst.

She turns to face me, steps into me and pushes to her toes. "Whatever it is, we'll get through it. And just to be clear. I'm already, most likely, probably, in love with you, but I won't admit it this soon."

Pri thinks she's in love with me.

There is a fire in the pit of my stomach and thunder in my ears.

She's giveth, and somehow, I know that gift is about to be taken away.

I cup her head and kiss her hard and fast when what I really want is to throw her over my shoulder and carry her to the bedroom. She trails her fingers over my goatee and then she's twisting away from me, already entering the kitchen. Adrenaline pumps through me, but I calmly follow her and soon we've reclaimed our seats at the island. The mood is decidedly somber.

Savage, Adam, and Lucifer are all in stony, unreadable soldier mode which in and of itself promises this is about to get nasty.

Fuck.

What the hell is happening?

Did Pri's family get hit? Surely not. They'd warn me. Did Ed get hit? Maybe. Fuck.

My eyes meet Blake's, and I say, "What the hell, Blake?"

And then he drops the bomb. "There's a warrant out for your arrest."

"What?" Pri gasps. "No. That would go through me. That's not possible."

"And yet it is," Blake says. "It's out of Chicago. The DA wants him brought in immediately."

"Chicago?" Pri demands. "You've got to be kidding me." She looks at me. "Have you ever been to Chicago?"

"Never," I say, my tone flat, while my mind rages with the regret of letting Waters and Deleon live.

"Well," she says, "that's where Logan is from. That bastard. What do they want to question him on?"

"A charge of murder," Blake states.

"Murder?" she gasps. "No," she says, recovering instantly. "No. He was an FBI agent. He has natural immunity. Damn it." She turns to me. "I'll fix this." She's already reaching for her phone.

I catch her arm. "Who are you calling?"

"Ed to start. Logan and my father are next."

"Wait just a minute, sweetheart," I say softly, blood rushing in my ears, while her eagerness to defend and help me is both expected and unexpected. The unexpected part being of my own making. "Blake," I say, holding her hand and eyeing him. "What else? Who did I kill?"

His jaw clenches. "Your brother while you were both undercover inside the Devils."

And there it is. Pri now knows my brother was an agent. She now knows he was undercover with me. I release her without looking at her and press my hands to my legs, but in my head, I'm screaming, Fuck, fuck, fuck. "What else?" I ask tightly, calmly even, despite the rage of emotions punching at me.

Instead of offering more details, he asks a question. "Was your brother ever in the state of Illinois?"

"No," I say, "at least not that I know of. This is Waters trying to discredit me as a witness. Obviously, we now know Logan's involved. Had I just jumped off this case, this wouldn't have happened."

"I'll handle this," Pri says again. "Let me do my job and protect my star witness."

I glance at Blake. "Let her do what she can do."

I grind my teeth and release her and she immediately eyes Blake. "Where is Ed right this minute?"

"He just arrived at the Walker facility."

"Then he had better accept my damn call because he should have stopped this from happening." She glances over at me. "I got this. You saved me, Adrian. I'm going to save you."

Only she can't save me. That sin will haunt me for the rest of my life. And hers, too, if I'm selfish enough to stay in her world.

LISA RENEE JONES

Chapter Twenty-One

PRI

"I need a minute," Adrian says, and then he leans on the island and stares at Savage. "If you let her do something stupid and get hurt, I swear to you, man, you think you're an assassin? I will be your assassin."

He's upset, a pulse of dark emotions radiating from him, but it's me he's worried about. I don't know one other person in my life who would put me first in milder situations, let alone one of this magnitude.

And for once, Savage doesn't snap back. "I've got her back," he says simply. "And yours."

And when Adrian's gaze slides to Adam, Adam concurs, "Make that two of us."

"Three," Lucifer says.

"Four and a whole lot more," Blake adds.

Adrian draws a deep breath, pushes off the island, and doesn't look at me. He just heads toward the stairs. I'm already dialing Ed. He answers on the first ring. "I need an all-inclusive immunity agreement for Adrian Mack and I need it now."

"I already know about Adrian Mack," he says. "Chicago is pressing murder charges."

"Aside from the fact that he has immunity while undercover—"

119

"Not as much as he did a few years back," he interrupts. "Not in the world we live in today and you know it."

"He's willing to testify on national television. His life will never be his own again, so don't counter with that, Ed. You should have already told Chicago this is bullshit. He's our star witness. Claim him."

"Murder, Pri. This is not a small charge."

"The Chicago team handling this is dirty," I say. "Waters got to them and this is all about discrediting our witness. I need the agreement for Adrian. And I need you to call Chicago and make this go away."

"I'm not dirtying myself up for a killer."

"A killer?" I demand, adrenaline surging through me, all but making my hands shake. "He's an FBI agent, a hero willing to give up his life to take down a monster. And I thought we were on the same team. I thought we all wanted Waters."

"I'm not giving him the agreement," he snaps. "Not until I see how Chicago plays out."

"Then he's not testifying," I say. "You get that, right?"

"Then I guess you'd better get to work making the case otherwise."

Unease curls inside me. This doesn't feel right. "What don't I know?"

"You know what I know."

"He's a member of Walker." I hit the speaker button.

"I don't give a fuck about Walker," he says.

My eyes meet Blake's and his gaze is downright cutting. "Then catch an Uber back to the airport," Blake says. "You're on your own."

"Who is this?" he demands.

"This is Blake Walker," Blake says. "I'm surprised you don't recognize my voice, considering I'm the one who set-up your protective service. You asked for my personal commitment to your safety."

"Right," Ed says awkwardly. "Blake. Of course."

"Right," Blake comments dryly. "Of course. Let me tell you something, Ed. Adrian is family to Walker Security. And since I'm not one to force a man to make a decision, perhaps our protective services have become a conflict of interest. You need some space between us and you to allow you to think with a clear mind."

"I sign your checks," Ed snaps.

"Walker doesn't need your money," Blake says. "I'm sure our references have made it clear how in-demand we are."

"Pick up the phone, Pri."

My eyes meet Blake's, anger in the depths of his stare that I feed off of, but Blake isn't done. "Ed," Blake adds, "I'll have my men get you to the airport when we hang up." Blake motions to the phone.

Understanding his cue, I punch the speaker button and go private with Ed. "Yes, Ed?" I ask.

"I do not like being cornered. If you want to keep your job—"

"You're threatening my job now?"

"Respect me. Keep your job. We'll be replacing Walker."

"Let me be clear with you, Ed," I say, "Agent Pitt was murdered in front of me. Someone set him up and planned to kill me right along with him."

"I heard. I liked Pitt. He was a good man."

"They will keep killing us off until Waters walks. And if you don't think you need Walker, then I question you in all kinds of ways."

"What the hell does that mean, Pri?"

"I don't need to spell that out. We both know what I meant. Do what is right or I swear to you, I'll go around you."

"You think it's that easy, Pri? The Governor is going to lose his shit when he finds out our star witness is being charged with murdering his own brother, a fellow FBI agent."

"If we lose Waters, the Governor might just lose his reelection. And if you let them drag Adrian through the mud like this, you're no better than Waters. Get me the agreement. Stand by your witness that I will personally vouch for. Do what's right, Ed."

He hesitates and then offers a partial concession. "I'll call Chicago and ask to see the evidence. Then we'll talk."

"There won't be any evidence. This is a fake plot twist. When can I count on you calling them?"

"It depends. Am I about to be out on the street?"

My eyes meet Blake's. "I'll ask Walker to give you the night to find another service. They're good men. They won't want your blood on their hands. I hope we're in this together, Ed." I hang up on him.

"You fought like a warrior," Adam comments.

"Fighting doesn't matter," I say. "Winning does."

"You think Ed's dirty?" Savage asks.

"I think Ed is weaker than I realized," I reply, stopping short of any agreement on that topic.

"Weak means susceptible to corruption," Blake interjects, his attention sliding to Lucifer. "What do we know about the trip his secretary took?"

"It wasn't some prize she won," he says. "Ed paid for it in full." He looks at me. "Was he afraid for her safety?"

"It's possible," I say. "But as you can tell, he's not a protective sweetie pie, either. And when he's busy, she's busy. With the Waters trial and election season, he's busy."

"Who's helping him while she's gone?" Blake asks.

"No one that I know of," I say, my brows dipping. "Which is odd, but Ed's whole decision-making process feels off right now. I've always felt like he was on the right side of the story, which is why I took this job."

"Well, so far," Lucifer says, "we haven't proven he's involved in anything nefarious. But we haven't even figured out how Pitt made the connection that got him in trouble last night, either."

"Waters is a man of resources," Blake adds. "He clearly has someone like us, even a team of tech whizzes working to cover up his shit. My concern with that is this: I'm someone who can track an electronic path. I'm also someone who can create a fake trail and make it look real."

I follow where he's headed with this and I don't like it. "You're talking about Chicago and fraudulent evidence."

"I am," he confirms. "My brother, Royce, and his wife Lauren are on their way to the airport now. Lauren's going to represent Adrian. He just doesn't know it yet."

"Is she good?" I ask.

"Damn good," Blake assures me, while the entire team chimes in with agreement.

I try to take comfort in the team's confidence but I don't quite get there.

"Royce was high up the FBI chain," Blake states. "He's well-connected there and knows a few people on the federal team handling Waters. That's why we knew Adrian was a good guy before we ever hired him. We're all well-connected to some pretty high places. We're calling in favors, and putting our resources to work, to get Adrian a federal pardon. We'll drive over or through Ed to get there if we have to, but whatever you can do, would be good because—"

"Any bump in the road," I say, "especially at the holiday, could delay the trial. Not to mention, if we don't get Adrian protection in time, I'll have to delay the trial anyway. We need him to ensure a win. And a delay could mean more people will die."

"Exactly," Blake concurs. "Pri, I know you need him, but we're talking about making him a hunted man the rest of his life. He needs to limit his testimony. Behind a closed door, off-camera, whatever you can do to limit him."

"You're right," I say. "You're right. I'll talk to the judge. And I'll see if we can arrange his sworn testimony sooner than later."

"Without him being arrested," Savage says. "If he goes to jail, he won't come out alive."

"I won't let that happen," I assure him and my gut twists with good reason—I know what I have to do. I know I have to make the choice between good and evil, right and wrong. And I know how close to home that hits. "Waters isn't sloppy," I say, glancing at Blake. "Do you have paper and a pen?" I ask.

Blake slides both toward me. I write down three names, names I've tried to forget, and pass the paper back to him. "Connect the dots to my father," I say, "and then I can make this Chicago problem go away."

Blake doesn't look at the paper. "You're going to threaten to expose your father's secrets."

"Yes," I agree.

"You believe he's in on this," he states, and it's not a question.

"I believe Logan's in on this," I confirm once again, not willing to believe my father would betray me, even risk my life. "But my father controls Logan."

Blake still hasn't looked at the paper. "You sure you want to do this?"

"It's painful," I admit, "but my father is not a good man. Adrian is. So, yes. I'm sure. Connect the dots and then I'll take it from there, but I'll need to stay here. At least for now."

He gives me a small nod and I turn away from him, walking toward the stairs. He calls after me. "Pri."

I pause and glance back. "Yes?"

"He *is* a good man."

"I know that," I say. "I wish he did, but I'm working on that."

I leave it at that and head down the stairs, eager to find Adrian. We are both broken and bleeding through the cracks our mistakes have created. I know this. I don't even try to run from this truth. I also know that broken people often erode within themselves, or into someone else. But maybe, just maybe, it doesn't have to go that way. Maybe a lucky few connect with the perfect soul, the one that heals them. I don't know which of these things awaits Adrian and me, or who we will become as individuals or as a couple. I just know that I need him. And he needs me. We need each other.

Chapter Twenty-Two

PRI

Once I'm downstairs, Adrian isn't in view and I don't know why I know he's in my room, but I do. Or maybe it's just wishful thinking. Hope. Me daring to feel hope. Whatever the case, I hurry down the hallway and when I enter the room, he's sitting on the bed, chin low. I shut the door and slowly his gaze lifts. He casts me in a tormented stare.

The air thickens with anticipation. Mine and his. I don't have to read his mind to know he's not in a good place, but the fact that he's here, in my room, tells me he's not pushing me away. This matters. This is progress. This is him telling me he's not walking away.

I hope.

I close the space between us and he watches my every step, the swoosh of a ceiling fan somehow louder now. I stop in front of him, and for several beats, we just stare at each other, a pulse of awareness between us. He seems to be waiting for me, and of course, why would he not? He made the first move. He came to me. He's waiting for my reply. Is he welcome? Do I still want him?

My hands press to his face and for a moment he doesn't react, but when I whisper his name, "Adrian," he seems to breathe again. His lashes lower, and he nestles into my palms as if my touch is everything.

I've never felt like everything to anyone.

He captures my hand and his eyes meet mine again, a punch of emotion between us. "Pri," he murmurs. "There are so many things you need to know."

"And you'll tell when the time is right. And I'll prove to you that I'm not fair-weathered. I'm not in this, any of this, most certainly, not us, because it's easy. But it is right and I'm not going anywhere."

"I'm not going to tell you that you're wrong. I don't think I have it in me to let you go."

"Good," I say, relieved that the tug of war is over. No more promises of hate. No more foreboding goodbyes. "Finally," I add. "And right now, I just really want to be with you. To be with *us*." I shove him backward onto the mattress, climbing on top of him, straddling him. "Don't let them win," I say, my hands on his chest, the thick ridge of his erection pressed to the hot spot between my thighs. "Don't let them make you believe you're like them. You're not."

He rolls me over, his leg sliding between mine, his big body pressed to mine, his elbow by my side, holding up his upper body. "I could say a lot of things right now."

"Should I say them for you? You're bad. Too bad. *So very bad.*"

"No," he says softly. "I'm not going to say those things anymore. You know. You don't care."

"Now you're starting to understand." My fingers curl on his jaw. "But just in case you decide to go down that rabbit hole again, I'm alone in a sea of sharks. Do you think you'll save me by walking away?"

His eyes darken, lashes lowering once more as he murmurs, "What are you doing to me, woman?" and then his mouth crashes down on mine, his tongue stroking long, deep, slow.

He lets me taste his anguish, pain, self-hatred. But there's more. There's his unyielding need for me and us. There is our unexplainable, impossible-to-deny bond. A bond it seems created in blood.

The kiss transforms and becomes another. And this kiss, this kiss is passion, so much passion, and tenderness. We savor each other, this time that somehow feels as if it's all the time we have, despite every promise we've made that there will be more, so much more. We undress each other. His T-shirt goes first, and my hands instantly seek the heat of his skin, the taut muscle of his hard body. I press him to his back again and he lets me, his body flexing beneath my touch, my mouth, my hands exploring his body.

My T-shirt goes next, and he does the same to me. Now I'm on my back and his mouth and tongue are on my nipples, teasing me, driving me wild. Soon we're naked in every possible way. I feel that. I feel how exposed and raw we are together and it doesn't scare me. We kiss. We touch. And when I burn for him to be inside me, plead with him even, he doesn't give me what I want. He slows us down. I'm on my back all over again and his hand is under my backside, squeezing as he nips at my lips.

"I need to know how you taste."

"I'm pretty sure you already know," I whisper.

"Not here," he says, brushing his lips over my lips. "All over. All of you."

And then he's sliding low, trailing his mouth downward to my belly, feathering kisses there, teeth scraping my hipbone, and sending shivers through my body. He owns me in this moment in time, and I don't try to hide it. I moan. I arch into his touch. I reach for him and the ache between my legs becomes almost unbearable.

And then he's there, right there, in the most intimate place on my body, between my thighs, his breath a warm fan on my sex, heat that promises all that I want, forever it seems. My fingers tangle in the dark soft strands of his hair, a silent plea. Almost as if that's what he was waiting for, his tongue flickers over my clit, a quiet touch there and gone that has me gasping, craving more.

"Adrian," I pant out, and then he's suckling me, drawing on me, driving me wild. His fingers caress the wet heat of my sex, and then they slide inside me, stretching me, stroking me. Sensation after sensation tingles through me, controls me—he controls me, while I have no control at all. The truth is that it's been forever since I've been so intimate with anyone and he is not just anyone. The room fades in and out, and too soon, embarrassingly soon, I tumble into release, shuddering against his tongue, my sex clenching around his fingers.

And when it's over, he's right there, sliding up my body, leaning over me, his mouth on my mouth, the salty taste of me on his tongue. He rolls us to our sides, facing each other, stroking the hair from my face. "I could die a happy man right now," he whispers.

"Don't say that," I chide, fingers tangling roughly in his hair. "You don't get to die. Ever."

His lips curve and he eases back to look at me. "Ever?"

"Ever," I repeat. "Never."

"I'm not going anywhere, Pri," he promises, kissing me again, our bodies swaying, a sultry, sexy dance that is so much more than sex. It's slow, it's somehow luxurious and dirty, all at once.

We ride that passion all the way to the shudders and shakes of our bodies, and then we collapse into each other, loose-limbed and sated. Long after the dampness has gathered on my legs, we stay there, just holding each other. It's Adrian, who moves first, kissing my head as he says, "I'll get you a towel."

Naked and oh so beautiful, he walks to the bathroom, returning quickly with the promised towel. He grabs his pants and pulls them on. "Just in case we have to move quickly."

"Right," I say, and I hate that he's right. I hate that we're in a safe house. It's a cold, hard return to the reality that people, perhaps lots of people, are trying to kill us. Some part of me, perhaps for the first time, fears that this is not a battle we can win. And yet, how can we afford to lose?

I quickly dress as well, and I'm sitting on the bed when Adrian sits down beside me, right beside me, our legs pressed close. His hand settles warmly, even possessively, on my thigh. "You're not swimming alone with the sharks."

Adrian is the first person in my life who has ever made me feel his presence, really feel it, inside and out. I touch his face, fingers trailing over his goatee, before sliding away. "You aren't either. You know that, right?"

"About that."

"I don't like how that sounds."

"I need to protect you. I need to protect Walker, which may require some distance."

"No," I say. "Absolutely not. Safety in numbers." I twist around to face him. "Lauren and Royce are on their way to Chicago, Blake is working on a federal immunity agreement, and I know Logan is behind this Chicago situation. I gave Blake three names to connect to my father. Once he hands me all the dirt on them, I can force my father to step in."

He tilts his head slightly, a pinch appearing between his brows. "Pri. Sweetheart. If this is that close to your family—"

"Then I have leverage."

"It's your family. Good or bad, family is family."

"Bad is the appropriate word and you know that by now. I know very well, and that's, as I said, leverage. I have it. And I'm going to talk to the judge and ask him to allow you to testify in private and early, for your protection."

"That won't be as effective."

"I have a strong case, just not strong enough without you. It'll be enough." My cellphone rings and I stand up. "It could be Ed. He was calling Chicago." I rush to the end of the bed where my phone seems to be, judging by the location of the ringing. Locating it, I quickly scoop it up, and frown as I spy my mother's number, though I'm not sure why. She calls. Not often, but she calls. The timing just feels off. A punch of unease follows that though, a very definitive punch of unease and I answer the call.

"Mom?"

"Pri, honey. Are you free for dinner?"

I glance over at Adrian. "Dinner? Tonight?"

Adrian stands and faces me, giving a shake of his head, as my mother says, "Yes. I was thinking of that little Italian place we both love. Just you and me. Your father's out of town."

That unease is back, nagging this time. "Where is he?" I ask.

"I don't know," she says, all nonchalant. "What did he say? Hmmm. Washington, maybe?"

"You don't know where Dad went?" I ask, and Adrian arches an eyebrow at that, confirming this sounds as ridiculous to him as it does to me. I grimace and add, "You are still married, Mom, right?"

"Oh, don't be dramatic," she snaps. "I trust him. We've been married a lifetime. And it's business. He travels often. Back to our dinner."

"I'm in the middle of a big trial," I say. "And in case you've forgotten, it's a dangerous trial. I have private security right now."

"Security is good. Bring them along."

My lips press together. She's stubborn, but that's nothing new. "Does this have anything to do with why Logan wants me to meet him?"

There's a dead, three-beat silence she ends by saying, "Dinner tonight, Pri." Her phone conveniently beeps, and she adds, "I need to go. I'll see you there at seven." She hangs up.

LISA RENEE JONES

Chapter Twenty-Three

PRI

The minute that call with my mother ends, I'm walking toward the bedroom door. Or I try. Adrian catches my hand and steps into me. "What just happened and where are you going?"

"My mother wants to meet. And my father is out of town. I'm assuming in Chicago. That means he's a part of what's happening to you."

"You don't know that."

"Oh, but I do," I say, and I can feel my heart thundering in my chest. And my chest is tight. The way it was when I was in that tunnel. I'm suffocating and this time in betrayal. "I feel it in my gut, Adrian, and my gut is never wrong. He recruited Logan out of Chicago. He's well-connected there. Logan wants to meet tonight, so he must be here, not in Chicago. I don't know why I didn't think of my father in the first place. And my God, how could you even consider falling in love with a woman whose father is trying to destroy you?"

He cups my head and presses his forehead to mine. "You are not your father." His hand settles on my face and he tilts my gaze to his. "And this Chicago thing is going nowhere. They have no evidence. I was never in Illinois. I know that. I stepped away from the kitchen just to take a moment to reason with myself. This is

135

how this went. Deleon told whoever is behind this to use my brother against me because he knew it would rattle me. And it almost worked, but even if I had to defend myself over my brother—"

"Stop," I order swiftly. "Stop before you say something you can't take back."

"You need to hear this," he insists. "I've never killed anyone that wasn't in self-defense, Pri. No one. That's not who I am. I don't know how the fuck I even forgot that fact. That's why I didn't kill Waters. And that's why, even when I could have claimed self-defense, I didn't kill Deleon."

"I know all of that," I say. "So does Blake. I'm just glad to hear that you're giving yourself that credit."

"Look, sweetheart, I know Waters. What he's good at is manipulation. He hits you where you're weak. That means, he'll come at me over my brother and you."

"Because I make you weak?"

"Because normal humans, which he is not, have emotional bonds. Those bonds make us stronger in most ways. However, it makes us vulnerable to monsters. That means he'll come at you through your family and me."

"And?" I ask. "Where are you going with this?"

"And we have to flip the switch and come at him."

"How?"

"I don't know yet. I need to think a bit. I need to talk to Blake." He strokes my hair. "Take a minute. Cool off. What you don't want to do is react to any connection you find to your family in anger. That's what he wants. And, sweetheart, you don't know how he might be manipulating those you love."

I inhale and let out a breath. "Right. That makes sense."

"Blake knows where your father is already. We'll go back upstairs, and we'll dig into a real plan."

I glance at my phone. "It's already two. How is it two? I need to call the judge and follow up with Ed. And damn it." My eyes go wide. "We just had sex, and I never took my pill. Please tell me it made it here." I dart for the bathroom and start digging through the bags Walker brought me, sighing in relief when I find my pill package. I pop today's dose out and down it, cupping my hand under the water to get it down.

I glance in the mirror at my smudged lipstick and quickly gloss my mouth. When I turn, Adrian's standing in the doorway, and I swear every time I look at him, he gets a little hotter.

"Everything okay?" he asks.

I close the space between us and press my hand to his chest, comfortable touching him now. That happened so fast. "The pills were here. I'm late taking it, but I'm sure we're fine. That's the last thing we need now. Me pregnant while we run for our lives."

He studies me, his lashes half-veiled, expression unreadable. "Do you want kids, Pri?"

I blanch with the unexpected question. "I don't know. I have a dysfunctional family and I don't exactly have the safest life. And I think I'm a bit jaded about the world I'd bring a child into, you know? I guess, maybe, probably, right now, I feel like I'm a no. What about you?"

"The same," he agrees. "It's been a long time since I thought about family in any way but the past."

There's something about the way he says those words, that has me asking, "And now?" and holding my breath while I wait for a reply, though I'm not sure why.

"And now," he says, "there's Walker. And *you*, Pri." He cups my face and leans in closer, his breath warm on my lips as he says. "I don't know where any of this takes us, but you are—"

There's a knock on the bedroom door and we both groan with the interruption of what felt meaningful, even necessary. A piece of a puzzle we are just fitting together, but that piece is now lost. "Sorry, sweetheart," Adrian murmurs, stroking his thumb over my cheek before he releases me.

He backs up into the bedroom. I ease around into the room as he opens the door, and while I can't see who's at the door, I hear Blake say, "Royce and Lauren want to get you on a Zoom chat regarding your defense in about fifteen minutes. Alone. I set-up the office upstairs for you. And I'd like to have a chat one-on-one. Also alone."

Adrian glances over his shoulder at me and I say, "Go. I'll be up soon."

He gives a nod and exits the room. He shuts the door behind him and I swear I feel it like a punch in the stomach. We've just sworn there is no goodbye coming. I know we both meant it, which is proof that we've come so far together, so quickly. But there is a truth here that we've just skimmed over because we want to be together. That truth is that my family being involved in this Waters issue—and they are—is a mountain of a problem. He says it's not, but when he thinks about this, really thinks about this, the reality of this development is cold, bitterly cold.

Anyone trying to get him arrested on false charges logically knows he won't come out of jail alive, and is, in my mind, complicit in attempted murder.

In other words, my family is trying to kill Adrian.

Chapter Twenty-Four

ADRIAN

I step into the office first, followed by Blake, and the only reason I notice the glass desk and a giant window with a view of the property is training and experience. Both have taught me to always know where I'm at and how I'll leave. As promised, there's a MacBook on the desk, ready for a Zoom call with Royce and Lauren, who is now my attorney. An attorney I need for complicated reasons that amount to my own decisions. Deleon and Waters are alive. My brother is dead. It's about as fucked up as it gets.

Blake shuts the door and I face him. "Where is Pri's father right now?"

"I see you figured things out," he says dryly, leaning on the door, and crossing his arms in front of him.

A muscle in my jaw tics at the easy confirmation that Pri's father is somehow involved in this bullshit. "He's in Chicago," I assume.

"No," he says. "He's actually in Houston meeting with an old friend from law school, a principal in the Milton, Murr, and Sheridan firm. Milton used to work in the DA's office and his ex-wife is a judge. Guess where?"

"Chicago," I supply.

He lifts a finger in my direction. "Bingo."

"Fuck." I scrub my jaw and walk behind the desk, pressing my hands to the surface, a roar in my ears. "Fuck."

"How'd you know?" Blake asks, claiming the seat in front of me.

"Pri's mother called and wants her to go to dinner with her. She told Pri her father is out of town and she couldn't remember where. Pri figured it out." I sit down. "Needless to say, she's freaked out. It keeps getting more and more personal for her."

"Not so personal that they know she's involved with you. Unless she told them."

"She didn't, but I'm not sure that would matter. I'm not sure they even care about Pri at all. That's how shitty they are. What kind of parent doesn't care about their child?"

"Too many," he says. "But I get it. I was blessed with good parents as well."

"There's a hit out on her. I hate to think they're involved. This dinner her mother wants to have. I don't like it."

"But it might be informative."

"I don't like it," I repeat.

"We'll protect her."

"I *don't* like it," I repeat.

"We need to know who our enemies are. So does she, especially if it's her family. And think about it. If Pri tells her mother she's seeing you, there will be a reaction, in the moment, and after the dinner. That might lead us to Deleon."

He's right. I know he's right, but he's also suggesting Pri become bait. "Would you want Kara to be bait?"

"Kara's an ex-FBI agent and a badass and the answer is no, I would not, but would I do it? I doubt I'd have a choice. Despite my objection, she'd make the decision for the greater good. In case you haven't figured it out, Pri will too. She's brave."

"She also has something to prove—that she's not her parents. I've been there in my own way, done that, and I'm living in the aftermath. I know how dangerous that can get."

"As do I," he says. "But there's no way to change her role in this. She's deeply involved, her family is deeply involved. This won't go away because she hides from it."

He's right but the problem is that it won't go away as long as Waters is alive. Why the hell I didn't see that in the past, why I thought the legal system worked with guys like Waters, I don't know.

The computer starts to buzz, telling me it's time for my Zoom call. Blake knocks on the desk. "I'll leave you to your meeting."

"You don't want to know what I'm going to say?"

"You said you've never been to Illinois. I believe you, therefore I've heard enough." He stands up and heads to the door, then glances back at me. "If you marry her, you know your in-laws hate you. The good news is that sounds rather normal to me."

He exits the office and shuts the door.

Married.

Me.

To Pri.

I wait for the rejection to follow, but it doesn't come. For the first time in my life, I've met someone who makes me want something lasting. But as long as Waters lives, I'll be hunted. That means she'll be hunted. And her family might not care about the danger they place her under, but I do.

I hit the answer button and bring Royce and Lauren into view. "Go ahead," Lauren, a pretty brunette, as feisty and strong-willed as Pri, says. "Tell us a joke to get this started. You know you want to."

Royce, a broody, bigger version of Blake, grumbles. "Yes. Get it over with."

And so, I do. "A penguin walks into a bar and asks the bartender. 'Have you seen my brother?' The bartender says, 'What's he look like?'"

I watch them stare at me for a moment while they catch on to the punchline—all penguins look alike. *But all monsters do not*, I think. All monsters do, however, die. In other words, maybe my version of being bad isn't bad enough.

Chapter Twenty-Five

PRI

Fifteen minutes after Adrian leaves me in the room alone, I'm dressed in battle gear. For me, that means a blue skirt and matching silk blouse, with a jacket and heels to complete the look. I'm driven. I have a purpose. I will win this war against Waters. *We* will win this war against Waters.

First things first, I grab my phone and listen to Logan's message again. "We need to talk. In person. It's urgent. Call me." His dogmatic insistence we meet doesn't feel off considering his personality, but something else does. I need to know what he knows, but a callback or my easy agreement to meet on my part would be what would be off. And it's late. I really don't have time to meet him today anyway, not if I plan to have dinner with my mother.

I shoot off a text: *We already talked. We don't need a repeat. And even if I wanted to meet, I can't tonight.*

Once I'm done with that, I call the judge's office and leave him an urgent message, during which Logan tries to call me. I don't take the call. I need him to work for this. I need him to react with agitation, which might make him say something he will regret and I can use it to help us in some way.

My phone rings again and it's the judge's office. I sit down at the desk and answer the line, "Ms. Miller?" a woman queries.

"Yes," I confirm. "This is her."

"I have Judge Nichols for you. Can I patch him through?"

"You can," I confirm. "Please do."

"Ms. Miller," Judge Nichols greets. "What can I do for you?"

"This is highly unusual and I recognize we'll need to schedule a time with opposing council—"

"But you're going to continue on anyway," he concludes.

"Considering I just spent the night hiding in a cave from an assassin, after watching an FBI agent get stabbed to death in front of me, yes sir, I am."

"I heard about your situation," he states grimly. "And I'm certainly enjoying, and I say that sarcastically, the unnerving need for security myself, which is why I returned your call promptly. Go on."

"Thank you, your honor. Our star witness is Adrian Mack, otherwise known as Adrian Ramos."

"Who I now understand has an arrest warrant in Chicago."

"Which is ridiculous," I say, barely taming the lift of my voice. "He's never even been to Chicago. This is a ploy by Waters to get him into a jail cell and kill him."

"Waters, who is in jail."

"Waters ordered that hit on me last night," I say, "which I know since the hitman told me. And," I add, "I might point out that even if Adrian lives to testify, Waters will be hunting him, if not directly, then through his people, for the rest of his life. We've lost witnesses, witnesses who were murdered, which is why I'm asking for permission to take his deposition now. If

144

anything happens to him, we need his testimony on file."

"A fair request the defense will argue against, but I assume you're ready for that confrontation."

"It's expected and yes, I am. I don't want him to testify in open court on camera, your honor."

"I'm certain the defense will have an issue with that as well."

"As I stated, I'm willing to argue my points formally."

"I'll authorize the deposition and inform the defense. No argument is needed. But that's to secure his testimony to be used if something happens to him. It's not a replacement for him taking the stand under oath in front of a jury. We'll schedule a Zoom meeting to argue that topic with defense, as I'm not prepared to see any of us dead on arrival to a meeting."

"Yes but—"

"We'll discuss with the defense."

My lips purse. "I'd like to take the deposition sooner than later. Our witness needs to be able to disappear and stay alive. As for open court, I'm open to arguments as early as this evening."

"Understood. Let's be clear, counselor, if he gives deposition and disappears, I may well throw out his testimony. I have not ruled yet on his dismissal from open court testimony. Am I clear?"

"Quite," I assure him.

"And I assume all of this means your witness is prepared to turn himself into the Chicago authorities?"

"He doesn't have a death wish, so no, I don't suspect he'll be turning himself in and I'm frankly hoping he doesn't change his mind."

"Are you telling me that you're harboring a fugitive, counselor?"

There's something in his tone that tells me he's going through the motions, covering his ass and mine. I offer us both said coverage. "I don't know where he is, though I have talked to him, but he contacts me. The depositions will need to be done via Zoom."

He's quiet, one second, two. "What else?"

I steel myself for a bad reaction and say, "I need to come clean on something."

"Is that right? Well, I'm all ears and listening."

"Adrian Mack saved my life at least twice now. I've developed a personal relationship with him. I'm hoping that won't be a problem."

"But you don't know where he is?"

"I was with him when I was attacked before either of us knew about the warrant. We were both attacked, but no, at this very moment, I do not know where he's at." *It's the truth*, I think. I mean, for all I know he's left the house.

"That's unexpected. I'll have to confer with the defense."

"They know. Waters knows. And he knows because his assassin was watching us. Consequently, I'm more of a target now because Adrian cares about me. Waters wants to hurt him hard and personally."

"I would think that would be a reason for you to want off this case."

"I would respectfully suggest that since I'm already a target, and I will remain a target on or off the case, that it makes sense for me to lead this war. Why delay the trial by replacing me when that just puts another life on the line? Not to mention that a delay allows Waters more time to arrange the untimely death of yet another witness and ensures that you, your honor, must continue to watch your back, quite indefinitely."

"Points well made. What does the DA say and why isn't he on this call?"

"He's presently settling into a safe house. We have reason to believe he's a prime target. A dead DA or—pardon me—judge, would certainly delay the trial, and really truly, who would want to start it all over again?"

He's quiet so long I start to fear we've been disconnected. And then he says, "You can stay on the case unless I see this personal relationship affect your performance. Now, again, what else?"

Relief washes over me. "That's it, your honor. I'll stand by for more arguments on Adrian's in-person testimony."

"Forthcoming," he assures me and disconnects.

I dial Ed and it goes to voicemail. Of course, it does. Waters got to him. I can almost taste it in the air. Thank God Waters hasn't gotten to the judge. My father is another story. I inhale and decide I've done everything but ask Blake where my father is right now. Almost as if some part of me doesn't want to know.

It's time, past time I find out and face the truth.

My stomach knots, but I stand up and head for the door. Once I'm upstairs, I find Blake at the endcap of the island with Adam in Lucifer's spot and Adrian facing me as I approach. Savage and Lucifer are missing. All three men stop speaking upon my approach while Adrian tracks my every step, his gaze sliding over my work attire—no, over my body. I halt opposite him and the moment my eyes meet his, I know my answer about my father. I know what's coming. "Tell me," I order softly.

He motions to the sliding glass door. "No," I say. "Thank you for trying to soften this blow, but just tell me."

"You know what I'm going to tell you, sweetheart," Adrian says softly.

"My father's in Chicago."

"In Houston, with a friend who's connected to everyone involved in the Chicago warrant," he supplies.

"I see," I say, letting that seep in, ice that burns. "Does he know he's involved with Waters?" I hold up a hand. "That's a stupid question for ten reasons, spoken by a daughter who doesn't want her father to be the asshole he is." I move on. "Okay. So, my family is involved. No wonder they wanted me off this case and didn't seek protection. Before we go further with that. The judge agreed to you giving your deposition via Zoom and he knows about us and he's approved me remaining on the case." I glance at Blake and then back to Adrian. "I'm still working on closed-door testimony."

"When is the deposition?" Adrian asks.

"I'd like to say immediately, but I'm sure the defense will argue against it, stall, and drag this out. And, of course, you don't have an immunity agreement. For that reason, I want you to talk to your attorney and of course, have her present for my questioning. If you're in agreement?"

"I am," Adrian states.

"Good. Now that we're past all that, how do we use me to end Waters once and for all?" My eyes meet Adrian's. "And don't tell me you won't use me. All the other people before us. We agreed." My cellphone rings on the island where I've sat it. I glance down and frown before my gaze lifts to Adrian's. "It's my father."

Chapter Twenty-Six

ADRIAN

Pri stares at her phone and I watch her perfect ivory skin, then flushes with pink. Her lips, also pink and glossy, press together as she decisively declines her father's call.

"Since I just made my relationship with you official to the judge," she says, her gaze lifting and finding mine. "I'd gamble and say my father just found out about us. Since we know Waters and his attorney already knew, I'd like to think that means he wasn't in the know for at least some things. For instance, the fact that Waters sent Deleon to kill us both last night." She draws a deep breath and inhales as she adds, "But I'm not going to guarantee it."

"You are not your father," I remind her softly, speaking to her concerns spoken in the bedroom, on the topic of her father's involvement with Waters.

"If your father just found out, Pri," Adam says, "are we thinking the judge is dirty? You did just tell him about you and Adrian."

"I don't get that impression at all," Pri replies, shifting her attention to Adam. "Quite the opposite, but I don't want to go down a rabbit hole of speculation. I wanted to wait to talk to my father until I talked to my mother, but I'll call him back and find out what he wants." She grabs her phone, punches the callback, listens a minute, and quickly says, "Voicemail, so we're back to speculation."

"And the judge," Adam replays.

"I'm on team Pri on the assessment of the judge," Blake says. "I don't believe he's compromised. He called the man I recommended for his protection, who is now in place. If he wasn't fearful for his life, I don't think he'd have hired him. If he needed privacy to work against the prosecution, I don't think he'd have hired him. And," he adds, "his electronic fingerprint thus far is clean."

"Then someone close to him has a big mouth," I assume. "Is that loudmouth a safety issue for the judge?"

"I've already alerted his security team," Blake replies.

"The judge called Waters' attorney," Pri says. "I'm sure of it."

"They already knew about us," I point out.

"Yes, but I don't believe my father did or I'd have heard from him," Pri counters. "The judge would have called the defense by now. I'd assume they felt they had to tell my father. Or maybe nothing we just talked about for ten minutes is accurate. My father was calling for another reason." She tries his number again with the same results. "Voicemail yet again," she announces, but this time there's a hint of relief in her, almost as if she'd hoped he wouldn't answer. She sets her phone down. "Moving on," she says, and her energy is jagged glass falling in shards around her as she glances between me and Blake and asks, "What does the FBI say about Pitt?"

"We're in contact and there's some chatter about him being dirty," he says, "but I find that hard to believe, considering he's dead." He glances at me. "What do you think?"

"I think Pitt was the only person who knew how to contact me while I was in hiding," I reply. "He has a whole lot of family that could be threatened. And he did surveillance on me and my brother's undercover operation. Maybe he heard my brother reference the cabin or even saw him go there. That's one option I hadn't considered. My brother went there while he was a Devil. And no one dealing with a Devil is ever safe, no matter what deal they've made."

"Including my family," Pri surmises. "I think I need to go by the office and keep the attention on me and Adrian, not my staff, thus my attire. Then I'd like to have dinner with my mother. However, I'd like opinions, please, from the people helping me navigate this while still breathing." She gives me a pointed look. "And before you reply," she adds softly, "everyone else before us. We agreed. Remember that."

I'm not sure I ever agreed to put her safety anywhere but at the top of my list, but I can feel her need to act, to do something, anything to make a difference. That need claws at her in a way that's all too familiar. "What do you believe you can get out of the meeting with your mother?" I ask.

Her reply is thoughtful and immediate. "The truly honest answer here is that she's my mother. I think I need to see her for some peace of my mind and I'm not even sure what that means. And outside of that, I hope for answers. She's no saint, but she's not my father or Logan." Her brows dip. "Actually, I sensed an urgency in her, almost fear. I didn't recognize it at the time, but right now, thinking about the call, I think yes, there was fear. Maybe she wants to warn me and with that warning comes critical information. Or maybe she needs help. I just don't know. The truth is, she could be afraid I'm screwing up her financial security."

There is bitterness and pain inside her words, layered beneath the logic and intelligence. Her family is not the loving shelter families should be, and despite all my trouble with my brother, I don't understand it. My family was a good family. Alex was an anomaly, troubled, and volatile.

"Then I'd say you should meet with your mother," I say. "We'll keep you safe. And her, sweetheart."

"I know that," she says. "I'm very lucky to be surrounded by all of you. She is, too, even if she doesn't know it." She clears her throat and straightens slightly, indicating the change of subject that comes with her announcement of, "I also need to meet Logan."

And so, the war begins. "No," I say. "Not Logan."

Chapter Twenty-Seven

ADRIAN

My rejection of Pri's meeting with Logan hangs heavily in the air, but Pri remains unfazed. "Why don't you ask me why I want to meet him?" she challenges.

"Well, I do want an excuse to kill him."

Something flickers, perhaps even softens in her eyes at my protectiveness but again, she doesn't back down. "That could be killing the hand that feeds us," she says. "I believe that in the right one-on-one setting, I can get him to make admissions I could record. Maybe big ones."

"No," I say, firmer this time. "You and him, one-on-one, in private, no. End of discussion. Not him. Give and take, sweetheart. You go to the office, you see your mother, you don't see Logan. Everything in my gut is screaming no on that one and it's not all personal."

"Pitt is dead. Witnesses are dead," she argues. "We almost died. We have to stop the bleeding."

"It never stops while Waters is alive."

"Then what is the point in all of this?" she counters.

"Hell if I know," I say. "That's a question we all should have asked when we went after him years ago and started this. What is the point? What is the endgame? What it isn't is you dead, Pri. Start with your mother. Decline Logan."

"Adrian—"

"See what your mother says," I continue, "and *then* decide what comes next. Isn't that fair?"

"Are you going to stay open-minded about Logan?"

"I won't want to, but yes," I agree. "I will."

The voicemail on her phone buzzes and she glances down at the log. "It's from my father. It's the first call. It's often delayed." She inhales and puts the reply on speaker. Her father's voice fills the line. "We need to talk, Pri. Immediately." That's it. There's nothing more.

"Well, that told us nothing." Pri comments, before she says, "What's our plan?"

"Lucifer will go with you to the office," Blake says. "I want you to leave him with your team and tell them he's a contractor hired to aid the investigation. He'll look for trouble and safety concerns."

"And when I leave for dinner?" Pri asks.

"Adam and I will be with you," I answer.

"You have a warrant out for your arrest, Adrian," she argues. "Don't you think certain forces might be luring you into the open where you get picked up and arrested? And don't you think now that they know we're seeing each other, they know that you'll be near me?"

Savage rounds the corner and jumps into the conversation as if he's been there the whole time. "Adam's a master of disguise. He's going to dress Adrian up as a chick. He'll be real pretty."

I ignore Savage. "No one but our team will know I'm present."

"If you're wrong," she says, "and you're arrested, no matter what skirt Adam puts you in, you're dead."

My lips quirk. "Rest assured, sweetheart, I'm not dying in a skirt."

"It's not funny."

"I'm not laughing."

"I am," Savage assures us.

Pri inhales and lets out a breath. "I'll get my things." She heads for the stairwell and I let her go.

I inhale and walk out of the kitchen, exiting to the patio, leaning on the balcony. I'm a bastard for getting close to her. She will never be free of Waters now, even if I walk away from her. The door behind me opens and shuts as Savage joins me, leaning on the railing beside me. "Jack and Jill went up the hill—"

"And I broke my foot up your ass."

"That doesn't rhyme."

"You sure about that?"

He scrubs his jaw and glances out over the horizon, his tone turning serious for once. "I fell in love with my wife when I was in med school and a new soldier, a young, good guy. Ironically, it was her father who dragged me into the assassin's life, which is a long story. Bottom line, I left her to protect her."

I glance over at him. "And?"

"And it still came full circle. I came back to save her and thank fuck she saved me in the process."

"What are you saying?"

"You might not be ready to admit it, but you love her. And you know it's too late to walk away. Adam will give you Captain America good boy advice which is fine and dandy. I use his moral half the time, anyway. Meanwhile, Blake won't say much because he knows he'd do exactly what I'm telling you to do."

"Which is what, Savage?"

"Stay. Destroy Waters. Better yet, kill him."

"You do know he's in jail, right?"

"Yeah well, sounds like a personal problem to me. Figure it out." He turns and walks away.

I stand there, staring out at the hill country that had once been my home, and a plan comes to me. One I think only Savage would approve of.

Chapter Twenty-Eight

ADRIAN

I don't linger on my plan to end this war, be it a right or wrong move. I know what has to be done. And I know I'm the only one who can make it happen. I'm the only one who can know.

For now, I head inside the house again, the entire Walker team present huddled together around the island to discuss the plan to protect Pri. Blake reviews logistics, in which we all argue, a normal part of our process until we settle on an agreed-upon plan.

That done, Blake moves on. "It's time to make a statement," he says. "Let's let Waters and his followers know Walker's here and we're ready for war."

"You sure you want to do that?" I ask.

"Loud and proud," he says. "As long as they believe they can intimidate anyone and everyone, the harder they'll stay on that task. Let's let them know we're here and invite them to come at us."

"They will come at you, Blake."

"Let's hope they do," he says. "Because we're ready. I already talked to Royce and Luke. We all say bring it." He motions to Lucifer. "I want you to make the staff working for Pri feel good. Claim your role as a member of Walker Security, not some random consultant she brought in."

"What about me going in with her as her bodyguard?" Adam asks.

"As much as I want to say yes to that," I reply, "Pri won't go for it. She'll fear it will freak out her staff. And frankly, I like you in the shadows. Waters' people will know she's got protection, but you, my man, are never easy to spot. You need to stay a surprise."

At that moment, Pri appears by my side. "Are we ready?" she asks, glancing up at me and I swear when those pretty blue eyes meet mine, I feel it in my chest. And right then, I have no idea why it's at that moment that I know, without a shadow of a doubt, that my willingness to do whatever it takes to protect her is not in question.

"Sidekick ready," Lucifer confirms, drawing her attention and offering her a mock salute. "I need to run and grab the car." He heads out.

Blake motions to Adam and Savage and they do the same.

Blake sets a small silver bracelet on the counter. "This is a recording and tracking device. We can hear everyone within several feet. We can find you if someone grabs you."

"Wonderful," she says, sliding the bracelet onto her wrist. "Nice to know you can find my body."

I give Blake a look and he quickly gets the message. "I'll give you two a minute. We'll be out front."

I step into Pri, my hand settling on her waist. "No one is going to grab you. We'll be with you and if I didn't believe you were safe, I'd be fighting you every step of the way. I know you know that. I am not going to let anything happen to you."

"I know," she says. "And that's a nice thing to know right now."

"Because of your father?" I ask.

"Because of a lot of things."

"Have you heard from him?"

"No, he hasn't called me back, but he may just need a private place to tell me how wrong I am to be with the likes of you."

My lips quirk. "Tell him you can't stay away. I feel too good."

Her cheeks flush a pretty, shy pink, but her words are bold. "You do feel good," she dares. "And why wouldn't I tell you or him that? For all I know, I won't be alive tomorrow. I'm not going to die with regrets, which is exactly why I'm not giving up this fight. Not for you or me."

My heart pounds for this woman and my hand cups her face. "And I am not giving up on this fight or you, Pri."

"My father—"

"I told you. He's not you."

Her cellphone rings and she reaches for it, removing it from her jacket pocket. I expect her father, but she gives me a shake of her head. "Logan," she says. "Should I—"

I take her phone, about to answer the call myself and say a word or two to Mr. Fucktard, as Savage would call him, but stop myself. He'll accuse Pri of harboring a fugitive. I decline the call and the front door opens and Savage calls out, "Get your asses moving, people!"

I slide Pri's phone into her pocket. She catches my hand and holy hell, it's such a small act that would mean nothing but trouble with someone else. With her, it's everything. "You don't think I need to see what he has to say?" she asks.

I force myself to consider that question objectively. "You really think you can get him to talk?"

"If I get him in the right place, at the right time, and say the right things, yes," she says. "I do."

"Which translates to what?"

"I'll tell him that I'm not dropping the case, nor coming back to work with him, and in fact, have a personal relationship with you. By phone," she adds. "I'll abruptly end the call. He'll seethe, seek me out, demand a meeting, and when he can't find me, he'll call again. I'll have to meet him, maybe at his house. He'll lose his shit. I may need rescuing, which I won't think too hard about right now because it's worth doing."

My brows dip. "Rescuing? Is he dangerous?"

Her gaze cuts away. "I think they're all dangerous," she murmurs, and when I catch her chin and direct her gaze to mine, she adds, "But you'd be close."

"Pri," I say softly.

"We need this to end. And no, he may not say anything that helps, but maybe he will."

"Like what?"

"Maybe he'll say enough for me to get my father out of the picture. I hate him right now, but unfortunately, I still love him, too. I need to get him out of the line of fire."

I hesitate, but how do I say no to such a plea? Why would I even try? "Then do it," I say. "Wind him up and then record him. I'll keep you safe."

She arches a brow. "You're going to let me meet him in person?"

"With me within reach," I say, "Maybe."

His lips curve. "Maybe?"

"Maybe," I concede. "Call him back."

"We want to wind him up. He needs to call me again. Then I'll do it."

My hand slides to her purse. "Is your gun inside?"

"Always," she says.

"Good," I approve. "We both need to know that you can blow a hole in someone's shoe, someone who might or might not be named Logan, and back him the fuck off if you need to."

Her lips curve, a smile in her eyes. "In his shoe?"

"Losing a toe freaks a person out. Never forget that."

"I'd laugh," she says, "but I don't think you're joking."

"I'm not," I say, motioning her toward the door and grabbing her briefcase as we pass the stairs.

The front door is open as we approach, and side by side, we step outside onto the porch. Lucifer is standing in front of a black convertible Mercedes, his ankles and tattooed-up arms crossed, his blond hair longer than usual.

He's a ladies' man, a player who showed those true colors the minute he was on scene but that's the way of a wounded warrior, with emotional baggage. That isn't what bothers me about Lucifer.

The truth is that I don't know why I resist Lucifer as a part of the Walker team when Walker accepted me freely. On paper, Lucifer's a better man than me, a pilot, ex-military, an agent of good, not evil. He's also the man who'll stand by my woman's side today.

My woman.

She is my woman, mine to protect.

Today that means it's time to trust Lucifer or reject him outright. And for once, where he's concerned, rejection feels wrong.

Blake trusts him and I trust Blake.

That means I need to trust Lucifer to keep her safe.

Good thing I plan to do just what Pri assumed I would: stay close to her, no matter what the risk.

Chapter Twenty-Nine

PRI

Lucifer is wearing jeans and a T-shirt, and somehow his attire, and that fancy Mercedes behind him, is meant to be a statement. I'm just not sure what. Adrian and I head down the front steps of the house toward Lucifer. "What's with the fancy car?" I ask, glancing over at Adrian, who has an edge about him that I'd call unusual, but perhaps it's not. How can he not have an edge? He just found out he has a warrant out for his arrest and that my father was involved.

I probably have an edge as well.

"I assume Blake wanted to make a statement," Adrian replies, confirming my suspicions. Lucifer and the car serve a bigger purpose than looking pretty. "One that says you're not alone," Adrian continues. "You have muscle and money behind you."

My brow furrows. "Does that matter to people like Deleon and Waters?"

"Until now, Waters believed you and I were just two lone warriors, surrounded by traitors, all of whom were loyal to him. Now he'll know we're surrounded by loyal, skilled, fearless soldiers."

Lucifer and Adrian exchange a look and Lucifer seems to take a cue and rounds the car, heading to the driver's side.

Adrian opens the passenger door and sets my bag on the backseat. I move toward the vehicle, even stepping behind the door, but I pause and face Adrian. "I'm thinking of our exchange a few minutes ago, about us not even knowing where this all ends or even how."

"Right now," he says, his hand settling warmly on my hip, "you focus on getting your family out of the way. Then I'll handle Waters."

Unease bristles inside me, and I narrow my eyes on him. "What does that even mean? You'll *handle* him?"

"It means I'll handle him." His hand falls away and I'm suddenly cold with his withdrawal, despite the hot day.

"What's going on with you, Adrian? What's in your head right now?"

"Funny thing is, Pri, for once, it's more about what's in my heart."

He means me. I see that in the warm chocolate of his eyes, but there is something more there, and that something more feels like a problem.

A white sedan pulls up behind us and he motions with his head. "That's my ride. Don't worry," he says. "I'm staying off the radar." When I think he'll turn and walk away, he steps into me, and then he cups my neck and kisses me. It's a wild kiss, a hungry kiss, a tormented kiss filled with secrets.

The secrets confuse me when they perhaps should not. I'm still waiting on that immunity agreement, but somehow it feels like more than that. It's too late for me to try to understand. Adrian's already walking away, his big, perfect body moving with lethal grace, a man with confidence and skill. A man who can kill but is so damn tender and sweet. I stare after him, confused, worried, twisted in knots.

I love this man. I know I do, but can I really confess that this soon? But how do I not? What if one of us ends up dead and I never told him? I touch my lips and it's almost as if his goodbye lingers in the aftermath of our kiss.

I launch myself toward him and yell, "Adrian!"

He halts and turns back to me. I'm in front of him in a heartbeat, throwing my arms around him. "I need to say something to you. Adrian—"

His hand comes down on the back of my head. "First this. I love you. I know it's crazy. I know it's fast, but I need to say it to you. And I need you to know I've never said it to any other woman." His mouth closes down on mine in a fast, hot kiss before he says again, "I love you."

My eyes burn for no good reason. "You kind of stole my moment. I ran over here to tell you I love you."

His lips curve. "Is that right?"

"Yes. I love you and I did say it to Logan, but I need you to know what I felt for him was nothing like this. It wasn't love. You are—"

A whistle squeals through the air, and Savage calls out, "Let's move!"

"Tell me later when we're alone," he says, his thumb stroking my cheek. "Be careful," he orders softly. "Because Lord help anyone who hurts you." With that, he releases me and jogs toward the white car.

Chapter Thirty

PRI

I climb into the Mercedes with Lucifer and shut the door. He lifts the roof and revs the engine, setting us in motion. "It's not flying a plane," he says, "but it will do."

"You're a pilot?" I ask.

"I am," he confirms. "If it lifts off, I can fly it."

"Then why choose Walker for a career?" I ask. "It sounds like you love flying."

"Walker has a fleet," he says. "And I run a lot of overseas missions."

"Adrian mentioned those missions," I comment. "They're dangerous, right?"

"They are, but they're also big money," he replies. "Walker makes us all millionaires."

"At what cost?" I ask. "Your lives?"

"We save lives," he says. "And Adrian did more than his share of saving people these past two years, or so I hear."

"He doesn't seem to like you much."

"So I noticed," he comments dryly. "But it's okay. I'd still take a bullet for the asshole."

"Why doesn't he like you?" I press.

"He doesn't know me and if I were him, I'm not sure I'd like anyone right about now. Even you."

"Me?"

"Everyone is on the take with Waters," he comments, pulling us onto a main road. "The fact that he just met you, you're this deep in the Waters case, and still, he's this into you. That's bigger than you realize."

"Yes," I agree simply, while Adrian's confession plays in my head. *I love you, Pri.*

He loves me.

Of course, I know that to some degree, Adrian and I are under duress. I know that means our love could be a façade, but it feels so damn real. It *is* real. I love Adrian, I do, good, bad, and all of him, though I know he doesn't believe that. Driven to protect him, I dial Ed and get his voicemail again. Irritated, frustrated, desperate for answers, my feisty side flares and I don't tamp it down. I mean, what do I have to lose? I text him: *I assume you're either on the phone or on your way to the airport again. I'd like to know which.*

I wait for a reply, staring at the empty message box, with as much patience as I have watching paint dry.

"Everything okay?" Lucifer asks.

"Just trying to get Ed to reply. Adrian deserves his immunity agreement and even that won't protect him. Waters' people could charge him in every city in the country and make him prove he's immune if they wanted to. It would be hell."

"And your father is one of Waters' people," he comments, no emotion, just unreadable matter-of-fact. "Any word from him?"

"No luck there either, but Logan called. I'm sure you know that since you're monitoring my communications."

"I did know," he confirms. "But it's always nice to know you're communicating with us."

I frown. "You don't trust me?"

"I believe you're an honest person," he comments. "Stuck between the man you most likely love and your family, who you will love, despite any and all abuse. That's just how life works. And that makes your decision-making complicated."

"No," I say. "I choose Adrian. I choose right over wrong."

He snorts. "And you think Adrian's going to beat Waters by being good?"

"Yes," I say. "Or no. I don't know. What are you saying?"

He cuts me a look. "Just asking questions."

My lips press together, not sure what to make of Lucifer. "I should tell you that Adrian and I agreed that I should goad Logan. He'll lose his temper and I know him. He'll admit something incriminating."

"Which does what for us? Because it damn sure isn't going to hurt Waters."

"I hope it allows me to force my family out of this," I say, feeling as if this explains my desire to break free of all conflict between my family and Adrian.

"And if it doesn't?"

My brows dip. "I don't know what you want from me right now, Lucifer."

"Again," he says, "just asking questions, ones I think you need to ask yourself."

My cellphone rings and I glance down to find a call from Logan. "Speak of the devil," I say, answering the call with, "I only have a moment. I'm about to walk into my office."

"What the fuck, Pri?" he demands. "You're fucking your witness?"

"Yes, Logan. I am fucking my witness." It's out before I can stop it and I glance at Lucifer, who's barely containing his laughter. "And you know what else?" I demand. "I can fuck who I want."

"He killed his brother. Are you insane?"

I smirk. "Talking points. All the talking points. You're almost a politician these days."

"He's trouble. Drop the case. Get out while you're still alive and if you do care about this asshole, he'll be free to hide again."

Again. That word sticks out to me for reasons I'll examine later. "I'm not going to drop the case. I have protection. I have Adrian. I have a mission and if it's the last thing I do, I will end the King Devil's reign forever."

"And if he kills you, Pri?"

"Is it me you're worried about or yourself?"

"This is bigger than you know."

"Actually, I think I know more than you think I know. I need to go. I'm walking into a meeting." I disconnect.

Lucifer laughs. "Holy hell, woman. If you wanted to get his attention, you just did."

Already my phone rings again and I glance down to find Logan calling. I decline the call and almost instantly it rings again. This time it's Adrian and I punch "answer."

"Weren't you supposed to agree to meet him?" he asks.

"Tomorrow," I say. "He needs to sleep on what just happened and simmer until he boils."

"Meanwhile you'll be fucking me?"

My lips curve. "Is that a problem?" I ask.

"Not even a little bit," he assures me. "I'll be ready to do my part." He disconnects and somehow, I'm smiling despite the fact that I just baited Logan. And I am perhaps one of the few people who knows just how volatile Logan can really be.

LISA RENEE JONES

Chapter Thirty-One

PRI

Lucifer pulls the fancy statement-making Mercedes into the downtown parking garage of the DA's office building and gets lucky enough to maneuver into a rare empty spot before killing the engine. In action mode, eager to do something, anything, that might affect this trial with Waters, I reach for the door.

"Before we go in," he says, halting my actions with words. "Let's talk about the plan."

"Okay," I say, settling into my seat again, albeit with heavy reluctance. The need to get inside and ensure no new bombshells have shown themselves is powerful. "What exactly is the plan?"

"I don't know if Pitt was dirty or not," he says, "but even if he wasn't, someone close to him set him up. That could be another agent, or since he spent a substantial amount of time with you, someone at the DA's office, someone here."

"Ed," I say. "I feel like Ed is dirty."

"Probably," he says. "But we were monitoring Ed last night. He was not the person who led Pitt to that cabin."

"Then someone else is dirty," I say, following his lead. "What do you need me to do?"

"Build up Walker, and our resources and skills, and do so in a big way."

My brows dip. "Won't that just encourage the bad egg to stay silent?"

"The bad egg is already silent, or we'd have found their electronic fingerprint. But when a person is pressured, they tend to panic. We want to set the fire and watch and see who tries to put it out."

"I've seen that in my work," I say. "That makes sense. Let's go set the fire."

"One last thing," he adds. "Assume there are recording devices all over the office, including on the people you're talking with. They might not even know it. Take nothing for granted."

"Right," I say. "I have to tell you, *Lucifer*," I emphasize the name as I add, "you Walker men are just bucket loads of warm, fuzzy comfort."

A few minutes later, Lucifer has been assigned credentials and a badge by security and we're stepping into the lobby. The receptionist, Shari, greets us, and she's all eyes and smiles for Lucifer, flicking her red hair over her shoulder and giving him flirty looks.

"Anything you need, Lucifer," she says, "I'll be your angel."

I roll my eyes and he and I head down the hallway. "Please tell me you don't get that often, though I suspect you do."

"Mostly in bed," he says, all matter-of-fact, like the comment is a simple conversation.

I'd comment, but Josh is walking toward us, and he's not with Grace as I'd expect considering he no longer works here and he's dating her. Next to him is Martin Morgan, a homicide detective that I'd last seen at Josh's going away party. I assess them, trying to figure out why the pair is here, and together.

Josh is classically handsome with brown hair, a man who, like Adam, you might call Mr. America, though more and more, I suspect Josh doesn't deserve such an honorable comparison. Morgan is blond and muscular, with a bit of a quiet bear personality. He doesn't say much, but what he does say is always kind of growly.

The four of us halt in the middle of the hallway, halfway to the conference room, deep in the bullpen of the DA's offices. Josh is directly across from me and I greet him first. "Josh, I thought we'd see less of you, not more now that you don't work here anymore." I eye Morgan and give him a nod.

Morgan lowers his chin in my direction and seems to ignore Lucifer.

"Grace has been freaking out about you," Josh comments. "You, Pitt, and the DA all being MIA has her uneasy."

"Me and Ed are not MIA," I say. "I told Grace what's going on."

"You know Grace," he says. "She's a worrywart. I came by to check on her and offer up my services again." He glances at Lucifer, or rather, pins him in a stare. "And you are?"

"Not your mama," Lucifer says dryly.

I have no idea what that means. Josh frowns and doesn't seem to understand either, but I have a feeling that's the plan. Lucifer wanted to put him off guard and I do believe it worked.

"Lucifer is the name," Lucifer adds. "Walker Security. And our services have already been contracted." He offers Josh a card. "Feel free to talk to our team about contract work."

Josh's face positively puckers and I do believe that's exactly what Lucifer wants. He doesn't like him. He's goading him the way I did Lucifer. Josh snatches the card from him a bit too abruptly. Lucifer's lips quirk with what reads as amusement. He then offers Morgan a card. "Detective Morgan," he greets. "If you need us, you know where to find us."

Morgan scowls, the scar on his lips protruding as he does. "How did you know who I was?"

Lucifer's reply is smooth and simple. "It's my job to know."

In other words, I think, *fear me. I see you. I see everything.* Lucifer is really good at this game, but then I suspect this to be true of all members of the Walker team.

"Did you need help with something, Detective Morgan?" I ask.

His gaze shifts to me. "I just ran a couple of cases over for Deanna. I'm just leaving." He casts Lucifer another quick, grumpy look and steps around him to leave.

Deanna is one of the ADA's who works with Morgan frequently. His story is believable, but somehow it just feels off. Whatever the case, I'm certain Walker will figure it out. I refocus on Josh. "I need to get with my team."

When I would step around him, he says, "Can we have a word?"

"I have a meeting soon," I say, thinking of the dinner with my mother while avoiding any conversation that might pin me in a bad spot. "Can you call me later? I mean unless it's urgent."

He grimaces and his expression takes on a bull doggish look before he concedes. "I'll call you." He steps around us and leaves.

"Dirty, dirty dog," Lucifer murmurs.

I glance over at him. "You think?"

"Oh yeah," he murmurs. "And I do believe it's time for me to meet Grace."

We start walking and I point a finger at him. "She's my friend. Do not lead her on, *Lucifer*."

He holds up a hand. "It's business, Pri. I don't play on the battleground."

Battleground.

God, that word, and the reality it represents.

Chapter Thirty-Two

PRI

Lucifer and I are still standing in the hallway, after our Josh and Morgan encounter, when I hear, "Pri!"

At the sound of Grace's voice, I turn to find her and Cindy rushing toward us, two beautiful girls, two targets for the devil himself.

Grace is quick to fling her arms around me. "I've been so worried about you."

"We texted."

"I know, but—" She pulls back and studies me. "What's wrong with Pitt? There are all kinds of rumors. He's dead. He's missing. And two federal agents dropped by to see you."

"Which happens often," I say, trying to calm her down. "It could be about Waters. Did you get a name?"

"No," she says. "They wouldn't talk to anyone else. They were at the front desk. There might be a card up front." She casts Lucifer a look. "Hi," she says. "I'm Grace."

And she's so sweet and charming, too. The girl next door, with cute dimples and all.

Cindy, who's more of a blonde goddess, and presently staring at Lucifer, cuts me a look. "Yes, Pri, what's up with Pitt, and who is the blond tattooed god you have with you?"

Lucifer laughs, a low, entertained laugh and I can almost imagine Savage and Adrian cracking jokes as they listen in. "Lucifer," he introduces himself. "From Walker Security, an international team contracted by the DA at Pri's request. We're here to assist with the investigation in an official capacity."

"We?" Cindy asks. "How many of you are there?"

"Unlimited resources," I say, following the plan. "Walker is quite well-known, sought out by heads of countries around the world. They've also taken our witnesses into their protective care."

"But why?" Cindy says sarcastically. "I mean, law enforcement was doing such a good job. *Not*," she adds. "Talk about a major fail that got people killed."

I motion them forward. "Let's head to the conference room and bring Lucifer up to speed."

Cindy smiles at Lucifer. "I'll be your guide."

Lucifer glances at me and I nod my approval. Cindy knows this case. She'll be a good, and obviously willing, resource for Lucifer. Now it's Grace rolling her eyes as she falls into step with me behind them. "Seriously," she says softly. "How are you?"

"Seriously," I reply. "I'm good. I've just had my hands full today."

"What's going on with Pitt?"

We pause outside the conference room. "The less you know right now, the better. Okay?"

Her eyes go wide. "Oh God. Is he okay?"

"I don't know," I say, but I do know. Pitt was hurt badly and at this point, he has to be dead. Doesn't he?

"That doesn't sound good," she says. "Please tell me if you get word on his safety. I didn't know him that well, but I knew him often. You know what I mean?"

"I know." I squeeze her arm and send her on her way, and since she's not part of this case, that means back to her office. Which brings me back to Josh. Grace isn't a part of this case and yet he used her to embed himself in the middle of everything. It could be about earning a paying contract, I know. But I'm back to yet something else that just doesn't feel right.

I head into the conference room and our entire team of twelve is assembled. The relief at my presence is palpable as Lucifer and I each claim open seats at the table, across from one another. Cindy, who is next to Lucifer at the table, introduces him and Lucifer explains his role. The moment he wraps up, Cindy asks, "What about Agent Pitt? Josh said he's missing."

Josh said, I think. Where did Josh get his information? The Feds? Waters? Who?

"That's true," Lucifer confirms, surprising me with his directness on the topic. "Former Federal Agent Adrian Mack, also known as Adrian Ramos, resurfaced and is willing to testify. There was a threat on his life and Pitt intervened. Mack is in hiding. Pitt is missing, but also severely injured."

"Wait," Cindy says, staring at me as the team murmurs wildly. "Adrian Mack surfaced?"

"He did," I confirm. "And he's a hell of a witness. He wants immunity and I'm waiting on that paperwork from Ed. The problem is that Chicago issued a warrant for his arrest for the murder of his brother."

The room erupts again and I hold up a hand. "We believe Waters is behind it. Mack was never in Chicago. His brother was undercover with the Devils as well and yes, he's dead."

"Walker is working on a federal immunity agreement for Mack," Lucifer adds, and then changes the subject, his gaze scanning the room. "What else did Josh tell you?" he asks, drawing Cindy's attention to him.

"Not much," she says. "He stressed the urgency to find him. That's what he's had our team working on this afternoon."

I sit up straighter. "Josh has been directing our team? On what authority?"

She blinks at me. "He said Ed's. I thought you knew."

Lucifer looks at me and then around the room, before he says, "Show me everything Josh accessed while 'helping' our team."

Cindy eyes me and mouths, "What's going on?"

My phone buzzes and I reach for it in my pocket, to find Ed calling. "I need to take this in private." I stand and grab my briefcase and purse and exit the conference room.

"What's the word?" I answer.

"Apparently you're sleeping with the witness, and I didn't know."

"Old news," I say. "The judge approved me remaining on the case."

"And if I don't?"

"We both know you need me. I'm standing out front taking bullets first." I change the subject. "What's the word on Chicago, Ed?"

Luckily, he moves on with me. "I can't get anyone to call me back," he grumbles irritably.

"Really, Ed?" I ask incredulously. "No one will call you back?"

"Pri, I know you don't trust me and frankly, I don't trust anyone either. Except for Walker," he surprises me and adds, "I've been with them for hours. Luke Walker specifically. Apparently, it's him, Royce, and Blake that run the operation."

"And what did Luke tell you?" I ask, entering my office, shutting my door, and rounding my desk.

"He shared Mack's history, including their profile before hiring him, as well as what he's done for them since joining Walker."

"And?" I ask, shoving my purse, which means my gun, in my drawer and setting my briefcase on the floor.

"I'll grant Mack the immunity agreement, but I think he needs the federal agreement Walker is working on. And even then, Waters could have legal teams stir up fake charges left and right until he gets arrested and ends up dead. If we can prove this case without him, he should walk away. And we should let him."

Unease rips through me. We should let him go. He should walk away. How convenient that is for Waters.

"I'll have the signed agreement scanned to your email in the next hour or two," he adds, and his phone beeps. "I need to take this."

"Wait, Ed. What agreement did you come to with Josh?"

"Josh? No agreement. I'm not paying him and Walker. Gotta run." He disconnects, and I'm suddenly extremely worried about Grace. And Adrian, because Ed is right. Waters will just keep coming at him.

My cellphone rings again and this time it's Adrian. I answer with, "You heard all of that?"

"Yes. I did. What does a liar do after he dies?"

My lips quirk. "I don't know. What does a liar do when he dies?"

"He lies still. Fuck Ed. I'm not walking away. I'm not hiding. And don't let him fuck with your head and make you think that's the right choice."

"And yet, you know—"

"I know this ends with me, Pri. And it *will* end."

"Is that supposed to comfort me?"

"Comfort isn't what you need."

"You are," I dare. "Maybe you should walk away, Adrian."

"I've already betrayed Waters. Because I choose not to testify, I do not get removed from his list of enemies. This is a battle to the end. It was always a battle to the end. Stay the course, baby. We got this."

Baby, not sweetheart, almost as if our declaration of love transformed his endearments. There's a new intimacy between us, even over the phone. "Yes," I say softly. "We got this."

"I'll see you soon," he promises and disconnects.

But as I set my phone down, I'm stuck on one point. Waters is in jail and still coming at us, most certainly at Adrian. He can get to us and we can't get to him. I think back to Adrian, his words "I'll handle Waters" and "this ends with me."

How does he think he's going to end this and why do I know I won't like that answer?

Chapter Thirty-Three

PRI

After hanging up with Adrian, I finally have the opportunity to investigate the FBI agents that visited me earlier. With my earbuds in place and phone in my pocket, I hurry up front and check-in with Shari. "Did I hear there was an FBI agent here to see me?"

"Oh," she says, brushing red hair behind her ear. "Yes. I do believe so, but they said they'd stop back by."

"Did they leave a card?"

"No, and we get agents around here all the time. I didn't think anything of it." She crinkles her nose. "Should I have?"

"It's not a big deal," I say, "but right now, with such a big case going on, I'd appreciate names and cards from visitors."

"Of course," she assures me. "I'll make sure. Sorry, Pri."

"Like I said, no big deal. Thanks, Shari." I quickly head back to my desk, sitting down and thrumming my fingers on the wooden surface, apparently still bothered by the unknown visitors.

Which is silly. As Shari stated, we have visitors, even agents, in here all the time. The timing is what bothers me, and not really even that. Pitt is missing. The FBI would have questions, but why not leave a card? Of course, Walker will have heard the conversations on the topic. They will have investigated. If there was a problem, they'd let me know. With that comforting thought, I set aside at least one worry, and dig into my work.

It's two hours after my call with Ed when the immunity agreement hits my email, but it comes with a catch. It requires an original signature. In other words, it feels like a setup. Like someone wants to ensure I lead them to Adrian. Or perhaps if I provide an original signature, I'll be exposed for aiding a fugitive, thus I'd be removed from the case. I was right. Ed is dirty. I'm angry and I decide yelling would be highly unprofessional. Since I can't talk to Ed without yelling, I text him: *Adrian Mack is not going to sign this agreement in person. Please amend.*

He doesn't reply. I decide yelling works for me. I call him and surprise, surprise, he doesn't answer. I leave the same basic message on his machine.

Frustrated, I grab my purse and decide to take a quick break to touch up my make-up before dinner with my mother, which is rapidly approaching. Heading to the lobby, I wave at Shari as I exit. "Quick freshen up," I say letting her know I'm going nowhere, since the elevators, like the bathroom, are also just off the lobby.

Once I'm inside the three-stall room, I step to the counter and unzip my purse, only to have my cellphone ring. Hoping it's Ed, I snake it from my pocket to find Adrian calling. "Almost done here," I say, answering.

"Not yet, unfortunately," he says. "There are two men that may or may not be FBI agents on the way up to your floor. The same two men we caught on camera about the time Shari claims two FBI agents came looking for you."

"They're not agents?"

"Unconfirmed. They may well be agents, but that doesn't mean they're not dirty."

"Because Pitt was an agent and he might have been dirty."

"Considering he's dead, I'd say someone close to him was dirty. We just don't know, Pri. Out of an abundance of caution, I'd rather you avoid these assholes until we have credentials and background. Stay in your office. Lucifer will meet them in the lobby. I'm headed to the back stairwell in case you need to leave quickly."

"Leave quickly? Oh God. That sounds bad."

"We're being cautious, that's all. If Lucifer gets a bad vibe, he'll send you to me to be safe. Just stay away from the situation until Lucifer gives the thumbs up."

"Yeah, about that. I'm in the bathroom right now. I'm right by the elevators. Do I have time to get out of here?"

"If you go now," he orders. "Right now."

"Going now," I say, shoving my phone back into my pocket.

With adrenaline pumping through me, I rush to the door, push my way out, and just as I would enter the lobby, Grace exits the elevator. She's holding four trays of coffee. "Help."

I hurry to grab a tray—because what can I do?—and I start for the door ahead of her. Cindy exits from the lobby right then and rushes toward us, blocking my path in the process. "There you are," she says, grabbing a tray from Grace. "You crazy girl, Grace," she scolds. "I told you I would go with you."

"You were busy," Grace replies from behind me.

Cindy is still in front of the door. Grace is now at my right.

"Pri."

At the sharp tone in Lucifer's voice, I intend to step around Cindy, but somehow Cindy precedes to literally spill the entire tray of coffee she's holding. I jump back and drop my own tray. It's a disaster. Cups slam to the ground and coffee splatters across the floor and all over my legs, thankfully missing my clothing. The elevator dings, two doors open and the two men, the "FBI Agents," both in basic blue suits, step out of the car.

I turn to face them. "Sorry. We've made quite the mess of the hallway. Can we help you?"

"Oh my God, oh my God," Cindy is chanting behind me. "How did this happen?"

"I'll get towels," Shari screams from the now open lobby doors. "Pri, don't step backward. There's a puddle."

"Pri Miller?" One of the men queries.

Thank you, Shari, for announcing my name, I think.

I could run for cover, I could. I know this and I would absolutely prefer Lucifer screen these men, but there are three innocent women fretting over coffee right here with me. I will not allow them to become targets. "I'm Pri," I confirm. "A little occupied right now, but what can I do for you?"

That's when I realize Adrian is still in my ear, "What the hell are you doing, Pri? I said to avoid those assholes, not talk to them."

Chapter Thirty-Four

PRI

The two men—aka "assholes," as Adrian calls them—step a little closer, too close for comfort. One is bald, forty-something, stocky. The other is taller, with dark, curly hair and hard features that include an incredibly straight nose. The tall one shuts the door. The shut door sets off alarms. I set my phone down.

"Agents Williams and Davis," the stocky one announces. "I'm Williams. He's Davis. We want to talk about Agent Pitt."

Lucifer steps to my side, ensuring I have a clear path to the lobby. "I'm Lucifer Remington, with Walker Security. I'm handling Pri's personal security. First and foremost, I'll need to see your ID."

Williams' lips pucker, but he reaches into his jacket and flips open his badge over to display his ID. Lucifer shoots a photo of it, before eyeing the other agent expectantly. The process is repeated.

Lucifer sends the photos to someone that I assume to be Blake.

"Can we go inside and talk a minute, Ms. Miller?" Agent Williams asks, giving me a pointed look.

"No need," I say, glancing over at Cindy and motioning her toward the office. She gives a nod and begins herding the other two women toward the door. Satisfied my staff are about to be out of the way, I return my attention to the agents. "Agent Pitt was working with me on a highly sensitive case, and as much as I want to help, that limits my conversational freedom, as you can imagine."

"When an agent is murdered, it's highly sensitive, *as you can imagine,*" Williams's snips. "He was a personal friend, Ms. Miller."

Adrian speaks in my ear, "He's telling the truth. He and Pitt came up together in the agency. They were friends. If one was dirty, the other might have been as well."

I'm still trying to process the implications of his words when Lucifer jumps back in. "Is this a personal or professional visit, Agent Williams?" Lucifer asks. "Because our team updated the FBI in lengthy detail last night when we realized Pitt was missing."

"We're aware of that," Agent Davis states, "but Ms. Miller failed to offer a personal statement. We'd like to know exactly what happened last night."

"Asked and answered," Lucifer quips.

Williams stares at him, his eyes hard before he looks at me. "I'd like to hear it in your own words."

"Leave me your card," I say, "and I'll arrange a time to sit down. I'm juggling the security of my staff and witnesses today."

"Yes, about that," Williams says, looking at me, "one of those witnesses is Adrian Mack. We'd like to talk to him as well." He glances between us. "Can either of you make that happen?"

"Fuck no," Adrian says in my ear. "I will not talk to that blowfish bastard."

With a solid no from Adrian, I reply a bit more delicately than he did. "Considering the fact that Chicago has issued a completely unjustified warrant for his arrest," I say, "I'm not even sure I'll hear from him again. In other words, good luck reaching him and as I'm sure the powers that be wished, my case is now in jeopardy."

"Unjustified?" Agent Williams asks. "How would you know that if you haven't talked to him since the warrant was issued?"

"Don't lie to a federal agent," Adrian says. "Not even for me, baby."

And I might have, I think. For him. Instead, I say, "I don't remember saying I haven't talked to him."

"Then you have talked to him?" Agent Davis presses.

"Yes," I say. "I have. And I fear every time he makes contact that it will be the last. And honestly at this point, if I were him, I probably wouldn't testify."

"Did Adrian kill Agent Pitt?" Agent Williams demands.

Adrian curses and I gasp. "What? No. He did not. He tried to save his life. Deleon killed Agent Pitt."

"We don't know if he's dead," Lucifer states. "Our team arrived and Deleon and Pitt were gone. And as I said, our team already covered this."

"Was Pitt there to arrest Adrian Mack?" Agent Davis asks.

"Why in the world would he arrest him?" I ask. "He had no known warrants at the time and the two were friends."

"Were they?" Agent Williams asks.

I hold up my hands. "Enough. I'm not on trial and neither is my witness. I'm done here."

"Can you come to our office tomorrow morning?" Agent Davis asks, in a rather oddly abrupt shift of topic. "Or perhaps we can come here? We can bring donuts."

"I'm not a cop," I say. "I don't live on donuts. And I'm waiting on a hearing with the defense and the judge that will likely happen in the morning. Give me your cards. I'll be in contact."

They hesitate and then Davis hands me his card. "Call me tomorrow or I'll be back to talk and I won't take no for answer." He punches the elevator button.

Lucifer motions to the office when Agent Davis says, "Ms. Miller."

"Yes?" I say.

"You do know that aiding and abetting is a crime, right?" He doesn't give me time to reply. "Of course you do. You work for the DA. And Adrian Mack knows that as well. He was, at some point, a federal agent, though I'm not sure he was ever a good one." The elevator opens and the two men step inside.

Lucifer's jaw sets hard and he motions me forward again. I don't say a word for fear of being overheard, but I'm fuming. *What the hell was that*? Lucifer opens the lobby door and I walk inside. Cindy and Grace immediately surround us. "What was that?" they ask as if they're reading my mind. "What did they want? Did they find Agent Pitt?"

"Come to the stairwell," Adrian says in my ear. "Now."

I eye Lucifer. "I need to—"

"I know," he says. "I'll update them." He glances at his watch. "You have a dinner to get ready for. Take the rear exit. I'll have a car waiting for you."

I don't think he knows Adrian is in my ear, and yet he's telling me to go to Adrian. He thinks those men were trouble and so do I. In other words, I'm just fine with going to Adrian right now except for one thing. He should not be in this building. What if this was all a setup and those men are trying to lure him out into the open?

Chapter Thirty-Five

ADRIAN

The stairwell door opens and I flatten on the wall behind the door, cautiously confirming it's Pri entering and not someone else. The instant she's in view, I grab her, pull her to me and settle her against the wall. "What part of avoid those assholes did you not understand?" I demand, catching her wrist and flipping off the communication device.

"I wasn't leaving my staff as targets, Adrian," she snaps, fiery as usual, but this is one war she will not win. "Would you really want me to do that?" she demands.

"Lucifer would have handled it."

"I had him with me the entire time." Her fingers curl around my T-shirt. "And what are you thinking? Why are you here? They were looking for you. *You*, Adrian, not me." She shoves on my chest. "We have to go. They could be coming for you."

"I'd know."

"Would you?" she challenges. "Do you think the members of Walker Security are the only smart people alive? Waters didn't survive this long because his people are dumb. I know you know that. I can't even believe Blake let you come in this building. And should we be in this stairwell?"

"I'm waiting for Blake to tell us we're clear to leave."

"Because we might not be?" she frets.

"We want Williams and Davis out of here for at least five minutes before we exit."

"Oh," she says. "Well then, back to what I was saying." She pokes my chest. "Don't be stupid for me, Adrian, or you will end up dead."

There she goes again. Worrying about me while I worry about her. I didn't want that for either of us. Not with my past. Not with my enemies. But it's too late. It's just too damn late to walk away from her. I don't even want to try.

My hand slides under her hair and I drag her mouth to mine, trying to have her see the logic I cannot. "I'm not the guy you fall in love with, Pri."

"Too late," she says. "We've already covered this. I'm not even going to try to pretend I'm not there yet. I am. I love you, Adrian, so stop doing stupid shit that will get you killed. Do you hear me?"

I laugh despite myself. "You're a bossy wench, you know that?"

"And?" she challenges.

"And this," I say, and my mouth closes down on hers, my hand sliding over her spine, molding her to me.

She is soft and delicate in all the right ways, but tough as nails. And she tastes like honey, thick and sweet with a promise of a better future, one I never dared to hope for. One I didn't even think I wanted. But I do now. I want her. I want that future *with her*.

Our lips part and my forehead rests against hers. "It's time to take a break, Pri."

She pulls back and gives an incredulous, "What? Are you seriously pushing me away right now, Adrian? Again? Because not only are you confusing me, I'm going to start thinking that's what you really want."

"Not from me or us, baby. We need to get out of town and lie low until we get a better grip on all the players. Give our team time to put control measures in place for the trial."

"But my staff—"

"We'll leave Lucifer here with a team," I say. "We need to do this."

"My family, though," she says. "I'm worried about my family. I know they don't deserve it, but I'm worried. I am. They're all I have."

"You have me, Pri. You have Walker."

"I know that," she says. "I do know that. I feel it, but they're my mom and dad."

"I know," I say. "My brother didn't deserve my worry either, but it didn't stop me from trying to get myself killed to save him. But he wasn't in danger. He was protected by Waters. And it seems your family is as well."

"But are they?" she asks. "If we disappear and Waters gets nervous, couldn't he use them to draw us out?"

And there it is. Exactly the problem I was planning to discuss with her. "Yes," I say, not about to lie to her. "Meet with your mother. Tell her just that if you have to. Even if your father won't listen, get her to agree to get out of the country. I'll pay for her to spend the rest of the year in Paris or Italy or wherever the fuck she wants to go."

"*You'll* pay?"

"I did a lot of tough jobs these past two years. What did I make the money for if not to use it now, when it matters?"

"My parents have money," she says softly, her fingers curling on my jaw. "But thank you. That means more to me than you can know. I mean, no one in my life has ever protected me, and my family doesn't even deserve your protection."

My hands settle on her waist. "Tell me you'll leave with me tonight after the dinner, Pri."

"And go where?" she asks. "New York?"

"Yes. New York."

"Won't everyone look for you there, considering that's Walker's home base?"

"Sometimes under their noses is the best place to be," I say. "And we have many resources in the city. If it gets too hot, we'll leave the country. So, I ask again—"

"Not tonight," she says. "I know my mother. I need to give her time to digest what I say to her."

"Pri, damn it—"

"At least overnight," she says. "Just give her until morning, Adrian. And then no matter what she says, or does, I'll go with you. I'm not an idiot. I was in a cave last night. I know we're in trouble."

Relief washes over me with her agreement and at the same moment, Blake speaks in my earpiece. "You're clear."

I hit the button to speak. "We're on our way, Blake," I say, and then disconnect. "Time to go." I catch her hand and kiss her knuckles. "I cannot wait to get you out of this city. Come on." I turn away from her, ready to guide her out of here when I have a realization. I think of what she said to me and how I responded.

I stop and turn back to her, molding her close again, tangling my fingers in her hair. "I love you, too," I say softly. "Don't forget that, Pri."

"I think I'm the one who needs to say that to you," she says, and I don't argue. I'm not sure love, new love especially, will be enough to get us to the other side of this. I'm also not going to pretend I don't hope it will, not anymore.

I kiss her hard and fast, and then I set us in motion, leading her out of this stairwell and, I hope soon, far away from this city.

LISA RENEE JONES

Chapter Thirty-Six

PRI

Once we're outside the building, we're quickly inside the SUV with someone I don't even know behind the wheel. "Mason," the driver offers, lifting a hand. "Flew in a few hours ago with a team of Walker men."

Meanwhile, Adrian is texting with someone and I just collapse on the seat, relieved to be in safe company. Relieved that Walker clearly brought in extra help.

Relief ends as we turn into another parking garage and I sit up, eyeing the tunnel we're winding a path around.

"Why are we here?" I ask, glancing at Adrian.

Adrian points out Blake standing next to a black sedan, and my shoulders slump with yet more relief. It's a hot minute before we're parked next to him. "Let's meet before your dinner," Adrian says, opening the door. He reaches over to me and touches my bracelet. "Best to turn that back on."

Blake joins us at the front of the vehicle next to the wall, where we stand out of view of pretty much anyone. "They're legit agents," Blake says. "Williams was friends with Pitt. Neither Williams nor Davis were authorized to question anyone on this case. They'll be investigated, but Williams' superior officer feels like he's just worried about Pitt."

I shake my head. "No. He was obsessed with Adrian. I'm not buying it."

"Me either," Blake assures me. "We have new men on the ground taking up residence at the prior safe house. We're in control, but Adrian's quest to get you both out of town is one I support. Tonight, after this dinner, is my preference."

"Tomorrow, please," I say. "My mother will not want to leave. I'll make my case, and make it firmly, but she needs time to process what I tell her."

Blake glances at Adrian who gives a nod. His lips press together. "I'll have the plane ready in case we need it tonight."

I hug myself with the ominous answer. "What do you know that I don't know?"

"I know exactly what you know," Blake replies. "Which is exactly why you should want to be on that plane tonight." He shifts the topic. "Adam and Savage are at the restaurant." With that, he walks away and clicks the locks to his vehicle.

Adrian steps in front of me, hands on my shoulders. "Mason will act as your hired driver. He'll be close. That means I need to ride with Blake."

"Please tell me that means you'll stay away tonight?"

"I won't be in the restaurant unless you need me."

"I won't need you. I have all your Walker allies. Stay away. It's just a dinner with my mother."

"We both know there is no such thing as just a dinner right now. Make this one as short as you can." He kisses me hard and fast. "I'll be listening."

I nod and he helps me into the vehicle, shutting the door behind me. Now I'm alone with Mason, and we're pulling out of the parking spot, on the way to my dinner with my mother. Adrian's right. It's not just a dinner. If it was, I wouldn't feel as if I'm headed to my execution.

It's a short ride later when Mason pulls us up to the restaurant. Thankfully he has a bottle of water and tissue that allows me to clean up my sticky legs. Even so, with the seat between us, I realize that I don't actually know what Mason looks like at his point. His hair is dark brown. His jaw has a several-day neatly groomed stubble, and when he glances at me in the mirror, his eyes are intelligent. "I'll be close," he states.

Words everyone keeps saying to me. Words that are both comforting and unnerving just by way of their necessity.

"I left my briefcase at work," I say. "Can you ask Lucifer to bring it to me?"

"Of course," he says.

"Thanks, Mason, and nice to meet you."

"Likewise," he says, in what seems like such a normal exchange. Oh, how I miss a normal life though I'm not sure what that means anymore. I'm not even sure I've ever known what that means.

I exit the vehicle to the slightly cooler night, still in the seventies despite the sun dipping behind the horizon and an early fall in the air. I cross the sidewalk to the restaurant entrance, a cute wooden door wrapped in ivy. My purse is on my shoulder, my gun inside, like a loyal friend who won't let me down. I step inside the cozy little Italian spot and the hostess greets me.

Soon I've discovered that my mother hasn't arrived, but we do have a reserved table. I'm guided through the small basic tables, the décor understated, as the food is the real star power of this destination. And I'm not focused on the tables or décor anyway. I'm people-watching, soaking in faces, looking for my would-be killer, though I'm not sure an assassin always looks like an assassin. Maybe they look like the elderly woman to my left eating alone? Or the incredibly large man in a fedora and glasses to my right, also eating alone, who's wildly familiar? Do I know anyone who wears a fedora?

Soon I'm in a corner spot that is thankfully one of the only private locations, considering the close proximity of the seating. I settle into the corner where I can watch for my mother. The man in the fedora is still bothering me and my gaze lifts and finds his. And I'm startled with recognition.

Chapter Thirty-Seven

PRI

The man in the fedora is Adam. My God, it's Adam. He really is a master of disguise. I fight a smile and relish a sense of relief.

I text Adrian: I *see Adam. I know you trust him. It helps to have him here.*

I do trust him, he replies. *More than I ever did my brother.*

It's a surprising confession by text, especially a text message I know Blake can read, but I have this sense of Adrian accepting the Walker team as a family in more than words. I believe their support—their absolutely committed support—has changed him in ways I might not even fully understand yet. But I want to understand.

And right now, Adam being here somehow places me just a little closer to Adrian. And he did say he'd be close.

The waitress appears, and with my mother nowhere in sight, I order us both a glass of wine, our favorite red blend to share, and then text her. While waiting on her reply I try to call Ed again. He doesn't answer. I text him: *Please call me.* A full two minutes pass with no reply, not from him or my mother. I'm not surprised by Ed's lack of response but my mother is another story.

It's not like her to be late and I text Adrian: *It's not like my mother to be late. Does Walker have eyes on her?*

She's at the front door now, he replies, *and she appears frazzled, though I've only met her once, so I don't have a lot to go on. However, Blake says based on the team's monitoring, she's definitely frazzled.*

It's at that moment that my mother rushes through the tables, dressed in a black silk pantsuit, her hair down, and somewhat in disarray. She's never in disarray, which set high standards for me I never quite lived up to as a child. Okay, as an adult either, but that's my own personal baggage issue.

"Hi, honey," she greets, and I stand up and she kisses my cheek and hugs me. "Thank God they got us this table. I hate being cramped." She sits down and hangs her purse on her chair right as the waitress fills our glasses.

"You have no idea how much I need this right now," she says, thanking the waitress and then me as she lifts the glass and sips. "I'm very stressed," she says, after a long, unladylike drink that is also so very unlike her.

"Why?"

"Let's order food. I need to eat something. I feel shaky. And let's get some of that yummy bread."

"Okay," I say. "Yes. I know what you like. I can order." I wave at the waitress, place our order, and we have bread pronto.

She quickly butters a slice and I do the same. "How are you?" she asks.

"I'm okay. You are not. What is happening?"

"I don't know. I mean, I do know. I thought your father was cheating on me."

"Oh. No. Tell me no."

"I did," she says. "I've spent a few weeks fretting over it. It's a big part of why I didn't leave the country. He urged me to go."

"You said—"

"I know what I said, but what was I going to say, Pri? I think your dad found a younger woman and I'm a washed-up old lady to him? It hurt, you know?"

"Of course it did, but you say it as if it's past tense?"

"Right well, I don't think he's cheating anymore. I'm actually thinking Italy sounds nice. Tuscany, maybe. Somewhere remote that I can just clear my head."

The food arrives and I draw in a breath. Something is wrong, really wrong. The waitress offers freshly shredded cheese and we both accept, each taking a bite of our food. My mother isn't looking at me and she picks up her wine and downs the rest of the contents.

"Do you know why Dad called me today?" I ask. "I can't seem to reach him."

"He called you?"

"He did."

"Well, he really wants you to come back to the firm, Pri. He's prepared to offer you your own division. Frankly, I'd like to beg you to accept. I'm so tired of all the criminals he represents. Maybe you can show him there is money to be made by representing innocent people."

"Since when do you care about innocent people?"

"That's horrible, Pri. You make me sound horrible. I stayed out of your father's business for a reason. I couldn't stomach it."

"And you like the money?"

"Of course I do," she says. "Is that a sin? I don't think so, but I'm not money hungry to the point of being blind. The truth is, I've always felt your father was a good man and I don't think I wanted to see him any other way."

I set my fork down. "What is going on?"

She sets her fork down as well. "I'm asking you to drop this case and come back to work for us. Just walk away now and maybe Waters will forget about you."

"Is Dad involved with Waters, Mom?"

She slides her plate away. "While snooping over the assumed affair, I overhead some things. That's why I wanted to meet here. I'm afraid our house is bugged."

"What things?" I ask, trying not to sound as urgent as the thundering of my heart suggests I am.

"Somehow, I suspect through Logan, your father got involved with Waters and is now trapped, held captive by that monster's demands. He can't get out and basically, Pri, honey, if you don't drop the case, they're going to implicate us all and send us to jail."

My eyes go wide and the room spins. "What? No. How do you know that?"

"I recorded a meeting your father had with some man I don't know. Your father never said his name, but he made it clear he didn't even know Waters was a client. The other man made it clear that the firm had laundered money for Waters for years now. Your father's implicated." She slides a tape recorder over to me. "Listen to it and drop the case, Pri."

Blood rushes in my ears. "I think you need to leave the country."

"I don't need to leave the country if you drop the case."

"And then what? Waters continues to control us if we don't stop him?"

"Maybe not," she says. "Maybe he'll move on."

"*Move on*? No, Mother. You're not being realistic. It's just a matter of time before he threatens us again."

"I told you," she snaps. "The man on the recording told your father that if you drop out of the case, Waters will free your father."

"Until he's not free," I say. "I'm going to get you on a plane out of the country in the morning. Pack a bag. I'll be by to pick you up."

"Dad—"

"Do not call him and tell him, Mom. The wrong people will find out. I'll tell him when he returns and try to get him to come and meet you. Okay?"

"I can't leave you and him here. I can't. What if something happens to you? If you two go, I'll go."

"Damn it, mom."

"Drop the case, Pri." She motions to the waitress. "We need to-go boxes, please."

"I'm leaving in the morning. I'll take you with me but you cannot tell Dad."

"No. I need to talk to your father. I'll meet him at the airport and talk to him."

"What time does he get in?"

"Four o'clock. Meet me here again tomorrow night. I'll try and get him to come."

"Okay," I say, though the agreement doesn't sit right in my belly. And I suspect it won't in Adrian's either. "I'll be here tomorrow night."

Chapter Thirty-Eight

ADRIAN

Blake and I are sitting in the back of a van, listening to Pri and her mother's conversation at the restaurant when the bombshell of her father's blackmail is delivered.

"Fuck."

It's the only appropriate word for what just happened, proven by the fact that I don't say it. Blake does.

Then comes her mother's insistence that Pri meet her for dinner tomorrow night when we're supposed to leave town in the morning. Followed by, of course, Pri's subsequent agreement.

"Fuck."

This time I'm the one cursing.

My foot starts to thrum on the floor of the van while I wait for the moment Pri and her mother decide to get their food to-go. Her mother leaves first and Pri lingers behind, ordering extra food that I know is for me. The very idea that she thought of me shouldn't surprise me, but then, it does and somehow makes this entire situation all the more combustible. I'm in this with her now. I don't want it to be any other way, but there is no denying just how dangerous this has become.

Eager to get to her, I reach for the door and Blake captures my arm. "No. You need to meet her at the house. Too many people are looking for you."

"Fuck," I mutter again because he's right and I can't protect her behind bars or dead.

I shift back onto the bench where I'd been sitting and stare at the damn ceiling without really seeing it, battling the rush of adrenaline spiking through me. "I know you just want to get her to safety," Blake says. "But you know you're going to have to kidnap her to get her to leave before that meeting tomorrow night. And that's not an answer."

My gaze collides with his and I snap, "Neither is her ending up dead, Blake, and I know you know that. Don't tell me if it was your wife, you wouldn't feel the same way."

"All right, then," he says. "What are you going to do?"

"Everything I can to keep her alive."

I don't say anything else. I don't have to. He knows anything means *anything*, and he knows he'd be in the same headspace if he were me.

The minute Pri is safely in the vehicle with Mason, she calls me. "I know you don't want me to stay," she says the instant I answer, "but they're my parents, Adrian," she adds. "And right or wrong, deserved or not, I love them. I can't make myself leave until I know what is really going on with my father. And before you say anything, before you object and I know you want to, can I just talk to you alone when we get to the house?"

"Deep breath, baby," I say, her torment a living breathing thing that is now becoming mine. Already

I'm mentally backing off my push to get her to leave tonight. In other words, this is me getting my ass kicked by a woman who is not even trying to kick my ass.

"I get it," I add. "All of what you just said. I do. I don't like it, but if it were my parents, I'd feel the same. We still have to talk about the right and wrong parts of this equation."

"Alone, please," she says again. "I don't want to get into a big debate with everyone involved until I talk to you and not because I don't like and trust every single last person on the Walker team. I'm just—my family and Waters—and I'm not in a good place right now."

Family. Waters. Two words together I understand. My mind flashes back to the past, to an image of my brother shoving a woman against a wall while she fought him. He was a devil then. He was with Waters and Waters is a devil maker.

With gritted teeth, I shove that little piece of hell away. "I think that's pretty normal under the circumstances."

"There's that word," she says. "*Normal.* I've decided I don't even know what it means, but it's kind of becoming a fantasy of mine."

"Normal is overrated," I assure her because she's not a person who would enjoy normal any more than I would. Otherwise, neither one of us would have done half the shit we've done.

"How about happy?" she asks.

"That's more like it." Right then, I know that is my new goal. To make her happy. But she has to stay alive to be happy and there's only one way to ensure that happens. I have to right a wrong of my past. Waters has to die.

"Mason's going to hand you off to Adam in a few minutes. Follow his lead and he'll keep you safe."

"Yes. Okay."

"I'll see you soon, baby."

"See you soon," she whispers.

We disconnect and she can't get to me fast enough.

Chapter Thirty-Nine

ADRIAN

I'm standing in the driveway when Pri arrives in an identical SUV to the one she'd ridden in with Mason, but now she has Adam behind the wheel. The instant the vehicle halts, the rear door pops open and Pri exits. She searches for me, finds me, and launches herself at me.

I meet her in the center of the steps and she throws her arms around me, pushing to her toes, reaching for my mouth, oblivious to the watchful eyes. And I for one, couldn't give two fucks about who's watching. I stroke her hair from her face and kiss her, a long stroke of the tongue before I capture her hand and kiss it.

"Let's go talk," I say and together we hurry inside and down the stairs. The instant I've shut us in her room—our room now—we come back together, mouths colliding.

I kiss her—how can I *not* kiss her, I'm addicted to her—feeding off her desperation, maneuvering her around and against the door. But still, I force my lips from hers and it's not easy, not easy at all when I'm hot and hard and just as desperate as she is. "Pri, baby, what is in your head right now?"

"You," she whispers. "I just want to feel something real and you're the only thing that feels real right now."

God, I am not good enough for this woman, but I'm going to be. I grab her wrist and flip off her bracelet even as I kiss her again and this time, I don't hold back. I drink her in, lick into her mouth, and take and take some more. And she does the same. I tug up her skirt. She tugs at my T-shirt. I pull it over my head and her hands are all over me, my mouth back to hers. One hand moves lower, to her panties, a finger sliding beneath.

She moans as my fingers caress her clit and sink lower, to the wet heat between her thighs. *So damn* wet and hot. My cock throbs and holy hell, I want inside her. I tear my mouth from hers, nip her lips and when she pants, I drop to my knees and drag her panties down her hips. She kicks them away and I turn her away from me, facing the door, unzipping her skirt and slipping it down her body. Again, she kicks it away—and fuck, her ass is perfect. I squeeze it, scrape my teeth over it, and another time, many other times, I'd linger to appreciate it, but not now. I turn her back around, my hands gripping her hips and my mouth pressing to her belly. She trembles beneath the touch and sucks in a breath with the lick of my tongue.

One of my hands caresses downward, and once again, my fingers press into the wet heat between her thighs. She moans softly, and I lick her clit. She pants and I suckle her, licking her, stroking her. Her fingers tug on my hair and I lift her leg, arching her into my mouth. There are women that give themselves to a man because sex is just sex, and I've certainly known my share. But Pri—Pri doesn't. When Pri, damaged, reserved Pri, gives herself to me, it feels like a gift to savor. And I do savor her, but not for long. She shatters in my arms and on my tongue, trembling all over, her sex spasming around my fingers.

And then she's whispering, "Adrian, I need—"

I lower her leg and stand, cupping her face. "Me, too," I answer, kissing her, letting her taste herself on my tongue, and that's all it takes to set us off again.

We're all over each other once more.

She presses her hand to my rock-hard erection and unzips my pants. I don't even know how it happens, but I end up on the floor, against the door, with her on top of me, riding me. I tug at her blouse, and in my eagerness to have her naked, manage to rip a button or two, but all she does is kiss me, and moan with my fingers on her nipple. I never get her blouse or bra off completely. She's just too good at making me feel good, swaying against me, meeting my thrusts, driving me wild.

When it's over, she collapses on top of me and for long seconds, a minute or two even, we just hold each other. "I don't know what to do, Adrian," she whispers.

I cup her head. "I know, baby, but we'll figure it out." I shift, help her up, and then stand up myself.

We end up in the bathroom, with her draped in a robe and sitting on the bathroom sink in front of me, my hands on either side of her. "Talk to me," I urge because I don't think right now is the time to tell her what I feel or what I want.

"I think Waters is winning, Adrian."

And she's right, I think. He is winning, but not for long.

"I think everything that happened tonight is for my benefit," she adds. "I mean, obviously it was since the endgame is for me to drop out. But I don't think Waters is threatening to take my parents down by way of exposing money laundering. I think he's letting me know how easily he can get close to them. How easily he can hurt them. How easily he can kill them."

And she's not wrong, I think again.

Waters has made his point. He's about to start filling body bags. Not that he hasn't already, but this time, they'll be people close to Pri.

Chapter Forty

ADRIAN

Pri and I remain in the bathroom, riding the high of sex, while the reality of choices that might mean life and death won't let us go. "We'll figure it out," I promise.

"I listened to the recording my mother gave me," she says. "It's in my purse, wherever it is. I think I dropped it by the bedroom door. It said just what she said. It was a quid pro quo. Get me off the case or else. I'd hoped I'd recognize the voice of the man threatening my father but I didn't. Maybe you will." She hops off the counter before I can help her and dashes around me and out of the bathroom. I follow her to find her at the desk, her purse on top as she digs through it.

"Bingo," she murmurs, holding up the recorder to show me before she sets it on the desk and presses play. I listen to the exchange between her father and this other man. The conversation goes as Pri and her mother led me to believe it would.

Pri watches me, hope in her face that I'll recognize the voice, I offer a negative shake of my head.

"Damn," she murmurs. "Damn it."

I close the space between us and grab the recorder. "Let me take this to Blake. Did you bring home food?"

"Oh yes. The food. I brought us food. I left it in the vehicle. Are you hungry?"

"Starving. I'll grab the food while I'm upstairs."

"And wine. There's wine. I thought we might need it and it's my favorite, actually. I wanted you to try it."

Because she is always thinking of me, and the truth is, she's risking a lot for me. It's not something I take for granted or take lightly. I stroke a strand of hair behind her ear. "Wine is good," I say softly, my heart so damn lost to her. She owns me and I don't even care. "I'll stop by the downstairs kitchen to heat up the food on my way back here."

"Sounds good," she says.

I kiss her forehead—I'm not sure I've ever kissed a woman's forehead, but then nothing is the same with Pri—and then head upstairs. I locate Blake at the kitchen island talking with Mason, who is a tall, muscular dude with lots of tats, dark hair, and a never-shaven jaw. He's about as new to Walker as I am but we've only crossed paths a few times. But I don't have to ask why he's here. I can guess. He's ex-FBI, and out of an East Texas office apparently, which makes him an asset. "Anything?" I ask.

"Nothing yet," Mason says, pointing at the bag of food and bottle of wine. "Except that, which smells damn good. You better take it and run or I will eat it."

"I'm still weeding through the security feed," Blake interjects, glancing up from the feed. "How is Pri?"

"Confused," I say. "And I don't really blame her. Right and wrong get real damn confusing right about now."

He arches a brow. "Are we leaving in the morning?"

"I'm not sure we know yet," I say. "Anything from the field?"

"Mason followed Pri's mother home after handing Pri off to Adam. She went straight there, no stops. He's headed back and we still have a man watching the house. Savage is following Cindy. He has some weird vibe about her."

"And Lucifer called," Mason adds, smirking. "Grace asked him to dinner."

Now my brows dip. "I'm confused. Isn't she dating Josh?"

"Apparently she needs to confide in Lucifer," Mason says sarcastically. "Lucifer's a lady magnet. I wouldn't count on that amounting to anything."

"And yet Grace isn't a flirt," I say. "She isn't one to go to Lucifer, the lady magnet, plus why not tell whatever this is to Pri?"

"We'll know soon enough," Blake says, moving on "I pulled a photo from the Millers' security feed." He turns his MacBook in my direction. "Know him?"

I study the tall, bald dude wearing a suit on the security feed. "No, and he's memorable. I wouldn't forget him if I'd seen him before."

"I'll text you a photo to show Pri," Blake offers. "And I'll get some facial recognition going on."

I set the recorder down. "That's what Pri's mother gave her. It's not overly helpful. And no, neither me nor Pri recognize his voice."

Blake inclines his chin and reaches for the recorder.

"Anything from Royce or Lauren?" I ask. Chicago now on my mind.

"A lot of bullshit," Blake says. "Lauren apparently started to curse when she never curses."

"Great," I say. "Just great."

"She's meeting the DA in the morning. More then."

I nod and head back downstairs. Pri, now in sweats and a tank top, meets me in the kitchen. "Anything else?" she asks. Her cheeks are pink and her lips swollen from my kisses.

The anything else I want is her naked and in bed again, but that will have to wait for later. "Nothing monumental," I say, unpacking the food and popping it in the microwave before setting the timer.

"Nothing from your legal team on Chicago? I just tried to call Ed again. I think I'm going to have to have Blake intimidate him again."

"Lauren's meeting with the DA tomorrow. Nothing good happened today. Nothing much but her frustration from what I can tell." I shift the topic. "Grace asked Lucifer to dinner, says she needs to confide in him."

Pri blanches. "What? I'm confused. Grace doesn't invite men to dinner and she tells me everything."

I dig around in the cabinet and find us glasses for the wine. "They aren't wine glasses," I say. "But they'll have to do. And maybe something happened after we left that set Grace off?"

Her lips press together. "It doesn't fit what I know of her. At all."

"Do you know this guy?" I show her the photo Blake sent me.

She studies it and shakes her head. "That's the guy speaking on the recording?"

"It is," I say. "I don't know him either. Blake will track him down."

"I could just ask my father tomorrow."

"You want to stay," I say, and it's not a question. I knew the minute she accepted the dinner reservation, her mind was made up.

"I promise to let you try and talk me out of it while we eat."

"And I will, Pri. You know I will."

Her lips curve. "I have no doubt."

She's smiling at this one but I'm not.

There's a ticking clock to that trial and the longer we're here in this city, the same city as Waters, the more we tempt fate.

Chapter Forty-One

ADRIAN

A few minutes later, Pri and I are side by side on the bed, lasagna, and wine in easy reach.

"This is my favorite Italian place ever," Pri says. "Well, in the States. I went to Italy a few years back. That's the best Italian food. Try it."

She went to Italy. Damn, I hate the clawing feeling that tells me it was with Logan. But I dig into the pasta and offer my easy approval. "Excellent. I approve."

She glances over at me. "I went with my mother. She was having some identity crisis."

"I didn't ask, but I would have. I'm glad it wasn't him."

"I wouldn't be talking about it if it was. He's another reason to stay. He'll confront me. He'll be angry and maybe he'll tell me something worthwhile."

Logan is the last person I want to talk about right now, I think, but I say, "I'll have to make you some of my mom's tamales for Thanksgiving."

"That was a dramatic shift of topic and I get the point. No Logan talk right now. As for the tamales. Thanksgiving?" she asks, sipping her wine.

"Yeah, baby. You think I'm going to let you spend it without me?"

"Good," she says, setting her glass down, her lips hinting at a smile, her eyes bright. "I want to try those tamales. Your mom must have been a good cook."

"The best. She was Mexican and my father was white, but you know that. My mom was a little thing with a big personality."

"You miss them," she observes.

"I do, especially at the holidays." I decide this is a moment to at least offer a little truth. "My brother, Alex, and I thought Waters had my father killed."

"That's why you both went undercover with the Devils."

"Yes," I say recapping at least some of what I told Blake. "We didn't tell the officials. We knew they'd say we were too close to the case."

"And did he kill your parents?"

"Someone working for him did. Ironically, Waters had the guy killed six months into my undercover work." I glance over at her. "I won't lie and say it didn't please me. But for Alex, it created some weird misplaced loyalty to Waters, and Waters didn't even know who the guy was to us."

"That's when Alex turned bad?"

"Alex was always a little bad, Pri. He wasn't ever right in the head. Dad and I knew. We always knew. We sheltered Mom from that side of him. And Raf was so much younger than Alex, he was spared at least some of Alex's shit."

"What does Raf think happened to Alex?"

"He believes he was killed while undercover, which isn't wrong. He was. And one day I really will tell him the story. He deserves to know. And so do you."

She strokes my cheek. "And when the time is right, you will." Her hand falls away. "Which brings us to now," she adds. "And why you can't tell me. Whether we leave tomorrow morning or tomorrow night isn't the real issue, now is it? If I drop the case, we could run away and hide for the rest of our lives, but I leave my parents at Waters' mercy. If I continue with the case through trial, they're at his mercy. I feel like a horrible person for saying this, but sometimes," she cuts her gaze, "sometimes—"

"Sometimes what, Pri?" I prod softly.

Her chin lifts and her eyes meet mine. "I wish you would have killed him."

I turn to her, hands on her shoulders. "I can't turn back time, but we can still end this."

"How?"

"Once I tape my testimony, killing me doesn't save him."

"Even if that's true, he'll be out in no time. You know that."

"And he has friends, I know enough to turn them into enemies. I'll make his freedom his nightmare."

"I—I don't even know if I can get that to fly. The defense will fight hard to stop that from happening."

"I'll make him take a deal."

"Sometimes it's safer in prison than out."

"I can't believe we're having this conversation." She scoots off the bed and starts to pace before she turns to me. "I need to talk to my parents, Adrian. I need to be sure we know what we're dealing with."

"Agreed."

"And we can't leave until I make the deal."

"All right then," I say. "It looks like we're staying."

Chapter Forty-Two

PRI

I wake to the pinch of light between the curtain, and the heat of Adrian's body where I'm nestled under his shoulder, on his chest. I'd revel in the feel of him close to me if not for the sudden voice at the end of the bed.

"Wakey wakey, love birds."

Adrian's head pops up. "What the fuck, Lucifer?"

I jerk to full awake mode and sit up, thankful I'm in Adrian's shirt. "What is happening?"

Adrian slides up the headboard, naked to the waist. "Damn it, Lucifer, can you knock? What if she'd been naked?"

Lucifer tosses a handful of peanut M & M's into his mouth. "Headed to the office early. Got in late. Thought you might want to hear about dinner with Grace." He motions behind him. "And I brought you your briefcase, Pri. I stuffed everything on your desk inside."

"Thank you," I say. "I really needed that."

"Are you seriously eating my candy?" Adrian demands.

"You always say it's the breakfast of champions," Lucifer claps back, and grabs another handful.

"Did she really invite you or did you invite her?" I ask, now fully cognizant. "And please tell me you didn't sleep with my friend and break her heart."

He finishes his candy. "I don't play where I work," he says. "We talked. She said Josh has been acting nervous and he took over the office today, which was out of character."

"Yesterday," Adrian says. "He took over yesterday."

"Right," Lucifer says. "Yesterday. She thinks he's being blackmailed to help Waters or some shit. I think he's dirty, but I can't find the electronic trail to back it up. We're taking a closer look at him."

"What about Cindy?" Adrian asks.

"Cindy?" I ask. "What about Cindy?"

"Sorry, baby," Adrian murmurs. "I forgot to tell you. Savage followed her. He got some vibe off her."

"Nothing to tell," Lucifer says. "She got takeout and went home last night. We're monitoring her calls now. I'll keep an eye on her." He glances at me. "I'm going to tell the team you have meetings and might be by later."

"Which she won't," Adrian says, and when my eyes shoot to his, he adds, "Quid pro quo, baby. We're not leaving town. I need you to limit your risk."

"Fine," I concede. "I'll work from here today. I have plenty to do before dinner."

"Then I'm off," Lucifer says. "I want to do a little digging around before the staff gets in."

He seals the M & M's and sets them on the desk, glancing back at Adrian. "In case you get hungry." And then he's gone, shutting the door.

I eye the clock that reads six AM. "I swear I need a run right now," I say.

Adrian pulls me beneath him. "This first," he murmurs. "Then we'll hit the gym downstairs in the basement."

228

I never get the chance to ask about that gym. He kisses me and I forget all about anything but him.

A few hours later, Adrian and I have worked out, had breakfast with the Walker team, while discussing all the moving pieces of well, everything, and showered. Adrian and I get ready after that shared shower together, which is really surreal. It's almost as if we can pretend that we're normal, and that armed men aren't roaming all around the house.

I dress for work, just in case I have to handle a problem, like a fight with Waters' counsel over Adrian. Today that means a navy suit dress with a fitted waist. Adrian is as hot as ever in black jeans, a black T-shirt, and boots, his goatee neatly trimmed.

It's mid-morning and I've set-up in the office upstairs when I get a call from the judge. "Your honor," I greet.

"The defense is being bullish about this in-person testimony. They say their client has a right to an open courtroom and a jury who is allowed to watch the questioning. They're not wrong."

"You're not even going to allow me to argue this with them?"

"I will, of course," he says. "But you're not going to win. I might want this to end, but I also have to do my job, and without bias. Do you want me to set a hearing?"

"Yes. Set it please."

We disconnect and Adrian, who's been talking with the guys, joins me, lifting his phone. "Lauren," he says, placing us on speaker phone. "I have Pri here, Lauren," he says, claiming the visitor chair across from me and setting the cell between us.

"Hi, Pri," she says. "Nice to meet you. I wish it was under better circumstances. I've never seen anything as dirty as what I'm dealing with here. No one is following the rules of the law. I can't get in front of the judge until tomorrow."

We chat a few minutes, all of us, and when we hang up, my gaze is on Adrian's. "The judge isn't going to grant you recorded testimony. I just hung up with him." I hold up a hand. "But before you go calling on Waters' enemies, let's talk about a few things."

"All right," he says. "Let's talk."

"For starters, there are two people who can undo this Chicago situation. My father, who we know is being blackmailed, and Logan. If we can trap him—"

"We can blackmail him?" he supplies, disapproval touching his brow. "Is that what you want to become, Pri?"

"Actually," I say, "I was thinking more like forcing his hand and garnering some kind of confession from him."

"What confession is he going to make that helps us and is worth forcing that confrontation on you?"

"If Logan pulled my father into this mess, he has to have a contact for Waters. That could be a member of Waters' legal team."

"We don't know that."

"It's a strong possibility," I say. "If we can prove Waters' legal counsel is dirty, they might force him to take a deal."

"How are you going to lead a conversation with Logan in that direction and get him to speak freely?"

"Just as I said before. He needs to be angry," I say. "Really angry. I have to push his buttons."

"Didn't you do that already?" he asks.

"I did, but he's shown remarkable restraint. I think I need to take it one step further."

"How?"

I snatch my phone from the desk and call Logan. He answers on the first ring. "Pri," he says icily. "Did you call to apologize?"

"I know what you did, Logan. I know everything and if you think I'm letting you take my family down, think again." I hang up.

Adrian leans closer. "Now what?"

"Now, we wait," I say. "He'll demand to see me and I need to agree."

"In public."

"My house," I say. "You can be there. Or that's probably not a good idea. Adam or Lucifer, or whoever you choose, can be there. Logan won't know."

He studies me long and hard, and when I'm certain he'll object, he finally concedes. "Your house," he agrees. "But if I get a bad feeling about this, it's off. Agree, Pri."

"I agree," I say, and the trap is set.

I just pray it's really us setting it.

.

Chapter Forty-Three

PRI

What I don't want to happen is for Adrian to get more involved with more people like Waters to destroy Waters. I know we're desperate, but I pray Logan represents a better way.

The problem is that Logan doesn't call back. I'm certain he's freaking out and doing damage control. But he'll call. I know he'll call. The day drags on though, and the call doesn't come.

By afternoon, I've chatted with several members of my staff, and Blake has yet to identify the man who visited my father. We all agree, I'll just ask my father. At five, I haven't heard from my mother and I text her to confirm dinner. She answers back immediately and says, *Yes. We're a go.*

Is Dad coming? I reply.

She doesn't answer. I try to call. She doesn't answer.

When dinner time arrives, Logan hasn't called and I'm a nervous wreck for no good reason. I'm just having dinner with my parents, or maybe just my mother. When it's time to leave, Adrian and I stand just outside the SUV that Mason will once again be driving.

"I'm nervous," I confess. "Why am I so nervous?"

"Don't ever ignore a feeling, baby," he says. "Be extra alert. Adam will be back inside the restaurant. I'll be around the corner with Blake and Savage this time. Mason will be out front."

"Okay." My hand settles on the hard wall of his chest. "I want you to know that if you ever give me the chance to love all the parts of you that you hate, I will."

His hand is at the back of my head and he brings our foreheads together. "Pri," he whispers, emotion, so much emotion, etched in my name. And then he's kissing me, a tender, passionate kiss that I feel from head to toe and right in the center of my heart. And I swear he settles right in my soul and nestles in to stay.

Reluctantly, we break apart and he flips my bracelet to on before I climb inside the vehicle. Mason turns on the radio, a mix of generations of music, and my mind floats back to the past. *I'm working late at the office, the only one there, and decide to make a pot of coffee. Once it's brewing, I leave it to finish, and I'm walking past Kelly Monroe's office. Kelly is a first-year attorney, young and pretty, a redheaded bombshell. The door is cracked and the sound of a voice murmurs low, almost rough. It's my father,*

"I told you not to do this," he snaps. "Don't cross me again."

"Or you'll do what?" Kelly demands. "Tell your wife on me?"

I suck in a breath and the voices just disappear. They say nothing more. Or I can't hear them. Afraid my father is coming, I hurry down the hallway and enter my office. I shut the door and start to pace, repeating Kelly's words: Or you'll do what? Tell your wife on me?

The SUV accelerates and I blink the present back into view. We're almost to the restaurant and an old Staind song, *So Far Away*, is playing. Kelly left the firm six months later and my father upgraded my mother's ring that year. I'd blown off that night, deciding it was work-related, but tonight, out of the blue, it's present again. I haven't been honest with myself. I know he had an affair with Kelly. I believe this memory is a reminder that my father is no angel, though I don't know why I need this reminder at all.

I know. I know so well. But he's not like Logan.

Mason halts us in front of the restaurant and glances back at me. "You good?"

"Better when this is over. And thanks for being here."

He gives me a shake of his head and I exit the restaurant. Soon, I'm sitting at the same table as last night, ordering the same bottle of wine. I scan for Adam and it takes effort, but I find him at a nearby table. This time, he's in a gray suit, his hair slicked back, and he's working on a MacBook. I sigh with relief just seeing him.

My mother is once again late and I text her. This time she doesn't reply. I try to call her. No answer. I try my father. No answer. I'm typing a text to Adrian when Logan sits down in front of me.

I blanch. "Logan."

His handsome face is flushed, as if he's rushed to the seat, or is simmering with red-hot anger beneath his perfect blue suit.

"Glad to see you ordered the wine already," he says, as the waitress fills two glasses.

My heart is thundering in my chest. "Where are my parents?" I ask, afraid for them, so very afraid for them.

"Your father told me to come get you in line."

Somehow, I manage to think straight and lower my phone to my lap to start the recording function because my anger snaps. "Get me in line?" I demand, leaning in closer and lowering my voice, though anger rips through my words. "You are the one in bed with Waters. I know what you've done. I know my father is being blackmailed and I know you're dirty."

"You know nothing," he bites out, "and stop being a spoiled little bitch trying to show off. Drop the case against Waters."

"I can't do that. The DA—"

"Will go along with it and you know it. If you drop it, he'll chicken out."

"No." My spine straightens, my chin lifting. "I will not."

"Do it or we'll all pay a price," he seethes.

"Maybe you just need to do a few more favors and make it all better."

"You will not fuck this up."

"Or else what?"

"Don't make me do something I don't want to do, Pri. Don't make me hurt you."

There's a bold, brittleness to that threat that sends a shiver down my spine. "This conversation is over." I grab my phone and purse and stand up.

He catches my arm. "Let go of me, Logan."

He glares up at me. "Fall in line, Pri."

"Never," I say, my skin crawling with his touch, and the truth is it's not the first time. "And let go of me," I order.

He seethes another moment and releases me.

Everything inside me tells me to get out of here, but when I turn toward the door, the bald man Adrian showed me on his phone last night is at the door. Adam stands and walks toward him. Adrenaline surges and survival mode kicks in. I detour and rush the other way, toward the bar and the back hallway that leads to the bathroom where I can lock myself inside. In the process, I unzip my purse, my hand finding my weapon. My heart is pumping and the distance I must travel is short but feels eternal. Finally, thank God, I'm shoving open the bathroom door, and just as I try to shut it, Logan pushes his way in.

The next thing I know, he's locked the door, and he's moving toward me, absolute poison in his eyes. I yell for him to stop, but he won't stop. He's here for a reason and it's not for a conversation.

THE END...FOR NOW

Adrian's trilogy concludes very soon in **WHEN HE'S WILD**! Be sure you've pre-ordered so you're one of the first to find out what happens when Adrian is faced with the devils of his past head-on.

PRE-ORDER HERE:

https://www.lisareneejones.com/walker-security-adrians-trilogy.html

If you loved the other Walker Security men, check out the other series from that world: Tall, Dark, and Deadly, Walker Security, and Savage's own four-book series—the finale in his series is releasing early next year!

Don't forget, if you want to be the first to know about upcoming books, giveaways, sales and any other exciting news I have to share please be sure you're signed up for my newsletter! As an added bonus everyone receives a free ebook when they sign-up!

http://lisareneejones.com/newsletter-sign-up/

The Brilliance Trilogy

It all started with a note, just a simple note hand written by a woman I didn't know, never even met. But in that note is perhaps every answer to every question I've ever had in my life. And because of that note, I look for her, but find him. I'm drawn to his passion, his talent, a darkness in him that somehow becomes my light, my life. Kace August is rich, powerful, a rock star of violins, a man who is all tattoos, leather, good looks and talent. He has a wickedly sweet ability to play the violin, seducing audiences worldwide. Now, he's seducing me. I know he has secrets. I don't care. Because you see, I have secrets, too.

I'm not Aria Alard, as he believes. I'm Aria Stradivari, daughter to Alessandro Stradivari, a musician born from the same blood as the man who created the famous Stradivarius violin. I am as rare as the mere 650 instruments my ancestors created. Instruments worth millions. 650 masterpieces, the brilliance unmatched. 650 reasons to kill. 650 reasons to hide. One reason not to: him.

FIND OUT MORE ABOUT THE BRILLIANCE TRILOGY HERE:

https://www.lisareneejones.com/brilliance-trilogy.html

***

GET BOOK ONE, A RECKLESS NOTE, FREE EXCLUSIVELY HERE:

https://claims.prolificworks.com/free/sYEuj2pM

Excerpt from the Savage Series

SAVAGE HUNGER · SAVAGE BURN · SAVAGE LOVE · SAVAGE ENDING

NEW YORK TIMES BESTSELLING AUTHOR LISA RENEE JONES

He's here.

Rick is standing right in front of me, bigger than life, and so damn him, in that him kind of way that I couldn't explain if I tried. He steps closer and I drop my bag on the counter. He will hurt me again, I remind myself, but like that first night, I don't seem to care.

I step toward him, but he's already there, already here, right here with me. I can't even believe it's true. He folds me close, his big, hard body absorbing mine. His fingers tangle in my hair, his lips slanting over my lips. And then he's kissing me, kissing me with the intensity of a man who can't breathe without me. And I can't breathe without him. I haven't drawn a real breath since he sent me that letter.

My arms slide under his tuxedo jacket, wrapping his body, muscles flexing under my touch. The heat of his body burning into mine, sunshine warming the ice in my heart he created when he left. And that's what scares me. Just this quickly, I'm consumed by him, the princess and the warrior, as he used to call us. My man. My hero. And those are dangerous things for me to feel, so very dangerous. Because they're not real. He showed me that they aren't real.

"This means nothing," I say, tearing my mouth from his, my hand planting on the hard wall of his chest. "This is sex. Just sex. This changes nothing."

"Baby, we were never just sex."

"We are not the us of the past," I say, grabbing his lapel. "I just need—you owe me this. You owe me a proper—"

"Everything," he says. "In ways you don't understand, but, baby, you will. I promise you, you will."

I don't try to understand that statement and I really don't get the chance. His mouth is back on my mouth.

The very idea of forever with this man is one part perfect, another part absolute pain. Because there is no forever with this man. But he doesn't give me time to object to a fantasy I'll never own, that I'm not sure I want to try and own again. I don't need forever. I need right now. I need him. I sink back into the kiss and he's ravenous. Claiming me. Taking me. Kissing the hell out of me and God, I love it. God, I need it. I need *him*.

FIND OUT MORE ABOUT THE SAVAGE SERIES HERE:

https://www.lisareneejones.com/savage-series.html

The Lilah Love Series

As an FBI profiler, it's Lilah Love's job to think like a killer. And she is very good at her job. When a series of murders surface—the victims all stripped naked and shot in the head—Lilah's instincts tell her it's the work of an assassin, not a serial killer. But when the case takes her back to her hometown in the Hamptons and a mysterious but unmistakable connection to her own life, all her assumptions are shaken to the core.

Thrust into a troubled past she's tried to shut the door on, Lilah's back in the town where her father is mayor, her brother is police chief, and she has an intimate history with the local crime lord's son, Kane Mendez. The two share a devastating secret, and only Kane understands Lilah's own darkest impulses. As more corpses surface, so does a series of anonymous notes to Lilah, threatening to expose her. Is the killer someone in her own circle? And is she the next target?

FIND OUT MORE ABOUT THE LILAH LOVE SERIES HERE:

https://www.lisareneejonesthrillers.com/the-lilah-love-series.html

Also by Lisa Renee Jones

THE INSIDE OUT SERIES

If I Were You
Being Me
Revealing Us
His Secrets*
Rebecca's Lost Journals
The Master Undone*
My Hunger*
No In Between
My Control*
I Belong to You
All of Me*

THE SECRET LIFE OF AMY BENSEN

Escaping Reality
Infinite Possibilities
Forsaken
Unbroken*

CARELESS WHISPERS

Denial
Demand
Surrender

WHITE LIES

Provocative
Shameless

TALL, DARK & DEADLY

Hot Secrets
Dangerous Secrets
Beneath the Secrets

WALKER SECURITY

Deep Under
Pulled Under
Falling Under

LILAH LOVE

Murder Notes
Murder Girl
Love Me Dead
Love Kills
Bloody Vows (January 2021)
Bloody Love (June 2021)

DIRTY RICH

Dirty Rich One Night Stand
Dirty Rich Cinderella Story
Dirty Rich Obsession
Dirty Rich Betrayal
Dirty Rich Cinderella Story: Ever After
Dirty Rich One Night Stand: Two Years Later
Dirty Rich Obsession: All Mine
Dirty Rich Secrets
Dirty Rich Betrayal: Love Me Forever

THE FILTHY TRILOGY

The Bastard
The Princess

About the Lisa Renee Jones

New York Times and USA Today bestselling author Lisa Renee Jones writes dark, edgy fiction to include the highly acclaimed INSIDE OUT series and the upcoming, crime thriller The Poet. Suzanne Todd (producer of Alice in Wonderland and Bad Mom's) on the INSIDE OUT series: Lisa has created a beautiful, complicated, and sensual world that is filled with intrigue and suspense.

Prior to publishing Lisa owned a multi-state staffing agency that was recognized many times by The Austin Business Journal and also praised by the Dallas Women's Magazine. In 1998 Lisa was listed as the #7 growing women owned business in Entrepreneur Magazine. She lives in Colorado with her husband, a cat that talks too much, and a Golden Retriever who is afraid of trash bags.

Lisa loves to hear from her readers. You can reach her at lisareneejones.com and she is active on Twitter and Facebook daily.

CPSIA information can be obtained
at www.ICGtesting.com
Printed in the USA
LVHW032129080321
680887LV00010B/2114

9 798579 828422